HOM FRIENDS 2
LIES OF OMISSION

DAWN DIVA

This book was written in its entirety by Dawn Diva for Ghetto Soul Productions

All characters are fictitious although some may be 'based' on people the author knows…

All rights to the Homies, Lovers & Friends series belong solely to Dawn Diva and Ghetto Soul Productions

Copyright © 2016 Dawn Diva

All rights reserved. No part of this book, except where permitted by law, may be used or reproduced in any way, shape or form without the express written permission of the writer.

Dedication

This book is dedicated to my children-DeAntre, Taji, Tyriq & Shamari and my grandchildren-Hasaan & DeAmonie. Y'all are my motivation, my inspiration...my reasons for fulfilling my dreams and continuously reaching, stretching and aiming for my goals. I know that if I develop the blueprint then I can give y'all something to follow. Never give up on yourselves or each other. I love you all...

La Familia.

Forever yours,

Mommy

Nene

D'igg

In loving memory of my nephew Larry Taron Maybank a.k.a. Tee

Shy Glizzy & Kodak we love y'all, keep ya head up ladies-Auntie D

Prologue

In book one of Homies, Lovers & Friends: The Beginning, it ended with Quade spying on Lainy & Shell. Here's a recap: Quade sat in the quiet of his private computer room with a dozen monitors glowing around him and watched Lainy and Shell's every move. He'd installed cameras all over her house before she'd even moved in under the guise of fixing up and painting the place. On another monitor the "betrayal" played out over and over again on loop. Not only had Lainy betrayed him for Shell but so had Keshunda he thought to himself while putting a bullet in the chamber of his glock 40 and cocking it back before aiming at the monitor that was on loop and shooting the image of a close up of Shell following Lainy down the hall, while continuing to watch the two of them. Since Shell couldn't take his eyes off Lainy's ass as she led him to her room, he shot him between the eyes, obliterating the harmless monitor into pieces. The rest of the clip was reserved for the on screen cast. He watched as Lainy kissed Shell on the lips, nodding her head in response to his question, he wished he'd added sound to the video as well so he could hear what they were saying too. But he thought he'd have time enough to do that later. Seeing them look at one another like long lost lovers made his blood boil. Bitch! If she thought she could get rid of him that easily after all of the time and effort he'd put into watching her every move, learning her routines and putting himself in situations where he could 'accidently' run into her, she'd soon find out differently. He'd been obsessed with having Lainy since he'd seen her at a friend's get together. They'd been introduced in a general sense but for Quin that was enough, he had to have Lainy by any means necessary. His girlfriend at the time didn't appreciate him eyeing and shadowing Lainy's every move. He even got close enough to listen to her various conversations with different groups of friends or individuals, whatever it took to learn something…anything about her. His ear hustle paid off when he heard her exchanging numbers with a potential client. Since they worked in the same field, computers, it would be easy to explain all of the weird run-ins. Slowly but surely he infiltrated her work life, getting a job with the same company she worked with and then personal life, making himself indispensable to her and playing the role of first co-worker, then friend and finally devoted boyfriend and fiancé all the while plotting on her for not giving into his sexual demands and feeding his insecurities to the point where he became obsessed with having her no matter what he had to do, but still wanting her to pay for making him feel like he wasn't worthy enough for her to share herself with him physically. He had been lucky if she even allowed him to kiss her every now and again, and any tongue was definitely out of the picture. Stuck up, man hating, black-hearted, frigid bitch, she was going to give him what he wanted and since she didn't want to do it the easy way, well then he'd just have to take it. Either way he was gonna permanently put his mark on her…figuratively and literally. No, Lainer Morrison hadn't heard or seen the last of him. She was going to rue the day she ever spurned the Quad.

Table of Contents

Dedication

Prologue

Closing One Chapter…

Opening Another…

Love Boat

Jokes On Who

Some Gets Some…

Some Gets None …

This Ain't No Game

Let's Ride

Getting What's Yours

In Need of Some Sexual Healing

Lies of Omission

Blood is Thicker Than Water

Good Cop Gone For Good

Vacay Baby

Star Board

Suspicions

Flying High

Getting Down Low and Dirty

A Devah in Control

Secrets Revealed

The End

Chapter 1

Closing One Chapter...

    Damn, I don't feel like this shit I thought to myself as I pulled up to the Miyabi Japanese Steakhouse & Sushi Bar on Citadel Haven Dr. to meet Tres and close this chapter in my life once and for all...at least for me. What Tres chose to take away from this was up to him, but for me it was the end of the road. As I drove through the parking lot I spotted Tres's tricked out, black & chrome Magnum parked by the entrance. I used to love driving that car when it was mine, but after that last stunt I gave it and everything else he'd ever given me back to him because I didn't want anything from him, point blank and the period...NOTHING. Him driving that car when he usually drove his Denali or Range meant he was trying to really get my attention, he knew I loved that car, but that's alright because what I was rocking with now was even better and luckily it had already been given to me before we'd broken up so he'd already dressed my baby up real good with all of the bells and whistles; butter soft leather seats with my name in the headrests, booming music system, TV's and DVD's, PS4 game system, scanners, EVERYTHING so I wasn't missing the Magnum as much as I thought I would but I still planned to get my own real soon and I would drop it right off to Drop ~N~ Top detailing & audio shop so Tres and his crew could hook it up real proper like. Sheeit I ain't crazy, that nigga did the best work in the Chuck and that's just what it is; besides I knew I would get a helluva discount. What? Don't judge me; I could definitely afford to pay full price for whatever I decided to get done but why? That fool owed me anyway for all the pain and suffering he put me through I thought pulling up next to his car. Just as I was getting ready to get out of my truck my cell rang. Not recognizing the number I almost didn't answer but something made me push the talk button.

"Hello." I said.

"What's up beautiful?" Ra's sexy baritone came through the ear piece giving me the shivers.

"Nothing much, who's this?" I asked fucking with him and wanting to see where his head was at.

"Yeah alright, play if you wanna but you already know. Anyway I see you made it to the restaurant in one piece." He said, shocking the hell outta me.

"What?" I asked looking around for the car I saw him driving last night. "You stalking me or something?" I asked not able to spot him.

"Yeah right, and you can stop looking around I'm behind you on the other side of the parking lot." He said flashing his lights. He was driving an old school gold Caddy. "As far as stalking you, you don't have to worry about that, but I do wanna make sure you're alright, even if you can take of yourself it would give me a piece of mind. So if it's alright with you I'ma chill right here until you're finished with your meeting."

"That's real sweet of you but as you've pointed out I am more than capable of taking care of myself, but if it makes YOU feel better than by all means do you." I responded shaking my head.

"I'd rather be doing you but in due time and what you over there shaking your head about?"

"You that's what and don't get cocky, doing me is a privilege that you may never receive." I told him anticipating his answer.

"You really DON'T know who you're talking to?" he responded after a long pause. "Because if you did, you'd know that doing you is a foregone conclusion and Devah…the privilege will be all mine for sure but the pleasure will be all yours." He said before hanging up. Damn, this nigga got me wet again I thought getting out the car and giving him the finger as I walked to the entrance. My phone goes off again and I retrieve the text message from Ra and read it: Wheneva ur ready I'ma do just that…this nigga makes me sick with his conceited ass, but if I'mma be honest about the situation, he turns me the fuck on. Got my legs trembling in these heels, knees about to buckle and my mind focused on the wrong things, which now that I think of it is precisely what he meant to do. Instead of being focused on Tres my mind was now on Ra…ooh that's some underhanded, lowdown dirty mess, but it worked. Tres was the last thing on my mind now as I spotted him sitting in front of one of those tables where the chef cuts, dices and cooks everything right in front of you while performing tricks. The things they could do always fascinated me which was why I loved coming here. I let the hostess know my party was already seated and head over to Tres looking forward to the show and the food more than the conversation.

****

I watched Devah as she pointed me out to the hostess and headed my way. Damn I missed the hell outta her I thought as I watched her strut over to the table, that walk she had was hypnotizing and I saw a few men get knocked in the back of their heads as they watched her walk over to me. I stood up as she neared the table and reached out to give her a hug, but she turned to the side before I could wrap my arms around her and it ended up being a half hug type thing which was better than nothing at all. I pulled out her chair and she sat down and hung her purse on the shoulder of the chair and turned her cell on silent which is something she always did when she went out to eat, her way of giving the other person her undivided attention. I guess that's a good thing considering she hadn't been giving me any attention since the 'incident' as I'd termed the reason she walked away from me and everything we'd shared.

"Okay, I'm here now so say…"

"Damn, I can't even get a hello before you start going in?" I asked throwing my hands up.

"My bad, hello Tres how've you been since the last time I saw you?" she asked sarcastically, "Now can you say what you need to say so we can both close this chapter in our lives and move on? Well you can anyway because I been closed it but if you need closure than that's cool, let's do this."

"That's real cold Devah, that ain't even you. Can't we just enjoy our meal and discuss our relationship in an amicable way?"

"WE don't have a relationship anymore. That's on YOU so don't sit there acting like you're the injured party here…this is your fuck up and if I'm cold towards you, well you did that too so deal with it. As far as the meal goes you already know I'ma enjoy mine, I love this joint." she said laughing at my attempt to guilt her. The look on her face clearly said 'Nigga please, that shit ain't even working'.

"I'mma give you that one, you right this is my fault but I'm trying to fix it, you won't give me a chance though."

"First off you ain't giving me shit, it was mine to begin with. Second, you've used up all you extra credits so right now you *dead* hombre, ain't no coming back." She said before placing her order.

"Damn Bae, straight like that?"

"Straight like that."

"Ain't nothing I say gonna change your mind huh?"

"How many chances did you have before then Tres, how many times did I forgive you for all the creeping and sneaking you thought you were getting away with? Why should I keep giving you chances to hurt *me* over and over again huh? Do I look desperate to you Tres, like I'm hard up for a man? Do I?" Devah asked in a controlled voice, trying hard not to spazz out. "They only reason, the ONLY reason you got away with all that shit you put me through was because you were my first everything and like a jackass I thought that meant as much to you as it did to me, but apparently not. But you know what, I ain't even mad at you, you taught me some very valuable lessons I plan to utilize in my next relationship and for that I thank you. And on the real, excluding your tricky dick, we had a wonderful relationship. You treated me like a queen for the most part, I mean we had our arguments and disagreements but that's normal for any relationship, we worked them out and moved on. I can't knock your love for me because I know you loved me in your own way but not enough to be faithful, your little head ruled your big one for the most part. But like I said you taught me a lot about myself, my body, how I should and deserve to be treated and about men, but what we had is over. I refuse to go back to that situation and be continuously cheated on and on top of that disrespected…"

"I never disrespected you D, wait I take that back I almost disrespected you once and that's when I tried to put my hands on you. Other than that…no."

"Oh so you don't think having people come tell me about what my man was doing with the next woman was disrespectful? How about when your little side chick was calling me from YOUR phone tripping and shit? Ooh wait, forget about those, I got one for you, how about when I came to your home to cook you a nice dinner and to chill with my man and spend some quality time, only to get there and find out that somebody else was already beating my time? And the worst part about it is you *knew* I was coming, granted it wasn't supposed to be 'til later but damn Tres in your home…where I had a key to come and go as I pleased? Really? You don't think that's disrespectful Tres?"

As I looked in her eyes I didn't see hurt or pain anymore, all I saw was disappointment and resignation and it finally clicked for me. I had lost MY first love, yeah I had love for Shy and Lex and I had a great connection…at one time, but nothing I shared with them could compare to what I'd had and lost with Devah. I knew then there was only one thing I could do for Devah, my biggest show of my love and respect for her and that was to let her go and so I did.

"I honestly didn't realize how much I was fucking us up D, I'm not trying to make excuses but that shit is so ingrained in me 'til I couldn't see what I was doing to you. I watched my mother go through the same thing with my father and to me it was normal si? She never left him, even when Cee had Nye she stayed and I guess I thought you would do the same. I apologize for fucking things up like that but more than anything I apologize for hurting you and putting you through all of that. I hope one day you can forgive me. And for the record, it meant and still means the world to me what you and I had together; *you* mean the world to me. You were my most perfect gift, my first love and I'll always cherish that, I just want you to know that." I said sincerely, a tear running down the side of my face as I fought to hold back the rest. Devah reached over and wiped the tear away, then wiped her own before standing up, stepping between my legs and giving me a heartfelt hug. Then she surprised me and probably herself by leaning close and giving me a deep, sweet and final kiss. When we came up for air she thanked me for my apology, the first one that had meant something to her and she forgave me. We enjoyed the show and the food, we laughed like old times, tripped on one another about shit we'd done or heard about the other since we'd parted…we shed some more tears, yeah I cried and I ain't a damn bit ashamed 'cause Lyfe said it best in his song 'Cry' it's like taking your soul to the laundry mat & ain't nothing strong about holding all that mess inside. But when it was all said and done we parted as friends and most importantly, on speaking terms. She even took me off the blocked list so now I can get through. No it didn't work out like I'd hoped but in reality it was better than I had any right to have hoped for. Life is good…God is good…forgiveness is good…friendship is better than the nothing I'd had and I now had all four in my life so…I'm good.

Chapter 2

Opening Another...

Ra sat in his car, his food sitting on the empty seat beside him as he replayed the sight of Devah wiping Tres's tears, hugging and worst of all kissing him as he stood there paying for the food he'd ordered from his phone while he waited on Devah to come back out, the scent of the food having finally gotten to him. The cashier brought him up out of his stupor when she repeated the total for his order. Ra turned away from the two as he handed the cashier his credit card and then signed his credit slip, adding a $5 tip before handing the receipt and the pen back, grabbing his food and heading for the door with all intentions of leaving the restaurant and going home. But he couldn't do it, instead after sitting in the car for about ten minutes, he decided to go back in and he asked to be seated at a small table where he could watch Devah and Tres. He ordered a drink and told the hostess he was waiting for someone so they would leave him alone to think. His mind couldn't shake the image of them hugging and kissing like long lost lovers, but there was something missing and as he replayed the image over and over again he realized what it was...passion. Tres looked more surprised than anything and Devah's body language was not screaming sex like it did when she was around him. It kind of looked like she was saying good-bye the way she was holding the sides of his face, but damn, that was one helluva good-bye kiss if that was what it was. After they parted she sat down and Tres ordered his food and they laughed and talked like two friends while the chef prepared their food in front of them, doing his signature performance for the repeat customers who specifically requested him whenever he was available, even if they had to wait. Ra was very intuitive and he soon realized that he'd jumped to conclusions and that whatever was said before he'd entered the restaurant to get his food the hug and the kiss was the culmination of it. Ra watched as Devah started hitting Tres in the arm for answering his phone, but stopped when she saw it was important. Tres ended his call and signaled the waiter over to the table for the check, Devah tried to tell him it was ok, she'd pay for it but he wouldn't hear of it. After loading his to-go box with his food he leaned over and kissed Devah on the forehead and wrapped his arms around her from the side in a friendly manner, resting his chin on her head with his eyes closed like he was in heaven. Devah reached up and placed her hand over his with one and rubbed his head with the other. I waited 'til he'd left before I got up to leave before she could see me, but then she turned all the way around and nailed me with a glare. As my waiter came over and asked if my party was still coming I received a text from Devah: U r TRULY stalker certified. U may as well come join me since Tres had 2go, I mean uv certainly spent enuf x staring ova here…STALKER!

    Laughing I let the waiter know that my party was already seated and went to join her.

    "How did you know I was in here?" I asked, I was pretty sure she'd never looked back to see me.

    "I could feel you burning a hole in the back of my head…I knew when you walked in the door. I don't know how but I did, it was like a change in the air or something." She said shrugging her shoulders,

"The point is I knew you were in here and that wasn't a part of our agreement. You said you'd wait outside, what changed your mind? Did you see what you wanted to see?" she asked tilting her head to the side and looking at me with her fork paused before her face. Damn she was gorgeous when she was angry.

"Calm down Ma, the only reason I came in was because the scent coming out of this joint was driving me crazy…I got hungry so I called in an order and when it was done they called me back and I came in and picked it up and had every intention of going back out to my car. Which is what I did, hell after what I saw, I almost left." I stated to which she again shrugged, I was really beginning to hate that shit.

"I never asked you to come to begin with." She said nonchalantly.

"Touché, but never the less I didn't leave because as I kept replaying it over in my head I realized something."

"Oh yeah? And what was that." She replied before taking a sip of lemon water.

"It didn't mean nothing. The hug, the kiss…none of it meant anything because there was no passion in it…at all. You didn't respond to him like you do to me so I saw it for what it was…a good-bye. Good for him but bye for you." I said laughing and finally getting her to crack a smile.

"So, how do I respond to you, because I wasn't aware that it was any differently from any other man?"

"Come on Ma…who you tryna shit huh? You know better than that so don't play yaself a'ight?

Granted I don't have anyone else to compare your responses to other than Tres and maybe your little honey from the party…what you call him? Shorty Do Wop?" he asked as they both busted out laughing, Devah almost choking on her food. She grabbed her neck and held up her other had to get him to stop so she could get herself under control.

"You dead wrong for that shit Ra, Mont is not my little *anything* ok?" she said after she'd gotten her composure back.

"If you say so, although I think dude would disagree with you."

"I'm pretty sure he knows the deal Ra."

"A'ight, I'ma leave that alone but back to what I was saying, I saw you with him and there was nothing there, even with that extra-long kiss you gave him." He paused for a few seconds side eyeing her, " Wait a minute you said you knew when I came in, did you do that so I'd see you?" he asked finally realizing the significance of the kiss…besides good-bye; she knew he was watching her.

"Ain't payback beautiful?" Devah smiled, her dimples sinking deep into her cheeks as Ra finally caught on.

"Payback for what?"

"Distracting me with your mind fuck before I came in here and for that text." Devah replied with a smirk.

"Oh you mean when your knees got all wobbly when you were on your way in the door?" Ra laughed.

"Oh you got jokes huh?"

"The funniest jokes are the ones based on reality," he said in all seriousness, "and the reality of the situation is that your body responds to me on a level you've never experienced before and I know that for a fact because you can't hide your reactions to me, they show on your face. I can guarantee dude can't make you as wet as I did with just words, I bet he can't make you forget what you wanted to say, make you do what you know you don't want to just because he said so, or make your legs so weak they can barely carry you…he can't but I can and I have and I'ma keep on doing it even more so when you become intimately acquainted with what your imagination couldn't even begin to dream of." Ra said leaning forward, his eyes shining bright and his words ringing with conviction. "You have no earthly idea what I have in store for you. I'ma make you forget every other man you've ever slept with, you gonna regret giving that pussy up to them other niggas when I get through with you." He said licking his bottom lip and leaning back in his stool, giving her back her space.

"That won't be hard to do." She finally replied asking the waiter for a to-go box as he refilled her water.

"Oh, so you know real when you recognize it huh?" Ra asked as she boxed up her food and stood up on shaky legs.

"No, it's not that. I've only slept with one person so I won't have anyone besides him to compare you to…seems we have that in common huh? You used him to compare my response to you and…*if* we move on to an intimate stage in this relationship…"

"Not IF but WHEN." He cut her off.

"Whatever…the point I was trying to make is that I would only have him to compare you to. Maybe I need to get some more experience so I can have something more to compare with. What you think?"

"Yo, don't play like that for real for real Devah, that shit ain't even funny, you shouldn't have even told me that shit. Wait are you serious? He's the only one you've ever slept with?" he asked incredulously.

"Yep." She responded before heading towards the door, leaving him staring at her ass as she strutted out the same way she strutted in.

"Damn, I gotta change my game plan." Ra muttered to himself, knowing she wouldn't be able to handle him like he needed her to. He was gonna have to break her in slow and easy. He just didn't know if he had the patience for it, but as he watched her look back over her shoulder at him before walking out the door, he knew he'd wait as long as he had to for his spoiled little diva.

Chapter 3

Love Boat

The CAILIN was making the rounds from island to island and the two families, their guests and crew all enjoyed the tropical two week holiday vacation from Antigua to St. Lucia. The yacht was like a home on water and had every amenity they could want or need. The crew was good at their jobs and most had been with the family since the beginning. The guests had only to ask in order to receive and were made to feel comfortable and pampered. From gourmet meals to spa treatments to entertainment, the CAILIN was top notch and the families didn't skimp on anything.

"This feels so good." Shane sighed in appreciation.

"Sis you ain't never lie." Devah moaned her own response.

The masseuses were working all of the kinks out of the women and earning every bit of their wages, not to mention the generous tips they always received from the pampered princesses.

"I am so glad I finally let your sickening ass convince me to come." Lainy murmured dreamily.

"What the hell ever." Devah replied. "If I had left it up to Shell he would've threw you over his shoulder cave man style so either way you were coming." She joked.

"That's what happens when you fall for an Actlin, they lose their freakin' minds when it comes to their women. Trust me I know, I'm engaged to one." Shane said flashing the huge, Marquis cut 4 carat diamond engagement ring surrounded by baguettes, Stance had surprised her with two mornings before on Christmas morning.

"Oh boy, do I need to put my shades back on?" Devah asked rolling her eyes.

"Aww don't worry, you can be next," Shane teased, "Ra is really feeling you, and come to think of it, we've both been so busy, I haven't had a chance to ask you how did it go when he came to visit you?"

This was the first time they'd seen each other since Shane's graduation party almost 4 months ago. As usual they went all out and Shane was given the royal treatment, the all-inclusive spa day Devah wrangled out of Stance, a complete wardrobe makeover from Londa & Ri and a brand new Lexus truck from Jace & Sean. Stance got her the Tiffany charm bracelet she'd told Devah she wanted with the matching necklace and Devah designed and created personal charms for her to add to them both like her favorite books, movies, flower, shoes, their zodiac sign and gemstone to name a few and had Talon, her employee and right hand not to mention a very creative and talented designer, to design a few exclusive shoes for her. Shell, Tre & CJ gave her the gift that keeps on giving…money and lots of it too. All the girls chipped in to send her and Stance to Cancun for a week. They'd had so much fun celebrating and catching up with one another that when the time came they didn't want to say good-bye. Since then Devah had been in Charlotte grinding hard, keeping in contact via phone, social media and

Facetime. She'd even convinced Lainy to come to NC to visit in October and stay for a week. They'd had so much fun. Talon showed them a wonderful time and his wife threw a cookout for Lainy so she could meet some of their friends and the part-time employee employed at Dripping Jewels, as they were definitely a close knit group. Lainy enjoyed herself so much she wasn't ready to go when the time came and promised she'd visit again real soon. About two weeks after Lainy's visit Devah had finally given in and let Ra come for a visit…by himself. He'd already been there with Stance and with Shell and Tre, but never by himself and Devah was a little…no make that a whole LOT nervous about his visit. She was at her store going over a customer's invoice and making sure everything was in order for the shipment when she heard the buzzer sound announcing that she had a customer in the store. Knowing that Talon hadn't arrived yet she welcomed the customer as she made her way to the front.

"Hello, welcome to Dripping Jewels." She said as she entered the showroom. "I'm Devah how can I…Ra! What are you doing here already? I thought you weren't coming until tonight." Devah said all in one breath.

"Well since you finally let me come without a chaperone, I decided to take advantage of my opportunity and get in as much time as I can before the real you takes over again and you send me home." He said with a smile.

"Screw you ok? No…I take that back 'cause I know you and you're about to totally run out with that one so…backsies."

"Backsies?"

"Yes, backsies. Meaning I can take that statement back AND you can no longer comment on it." She said looking him in the eyes as she told him the rules to her version of 'backsies', serious as all get out.

"Really Devah? Please tell me you just made that shit up." Ra said, as he reached for her. "Can I get a hug, a kiss, both…*something*?"

Devah walked over to him, hips swaying seductively, naturally and he wrapped her in his arms before leaning down for a kiss. Ra nibbled on Devah's bottom lip as he rubbed his hands up and down her back.

"You feel so good in my arms, I miss you Boo. Texting, Facetiming and talking on the phone ain't doing it for me. I need to be able to see you, hold you…kiss you." Ra said before one hand settled on her ass and the other to the back of her head tilting it to the right angle and kissing her with so much passion there was no mistaking what else he wanted to do and if that wasn't enough, his thick arousal pressing into her left no doubt. Devah moaned as their tongues danced together and they sucked and nibbled on each other's tongue and lips. Ra lifted Devah up and sat her on the counter and she wrapped her legs around him. Ra unbuttoned the top three buttons on her button down shirt and reached in to caress her breast and lightly pinch on her nipples as he kissed his way down her neck. Devah pushed her breast in his hands, moaning and grinding on his hardness losing her mind and all sense of awareness of her surroundings. Devah tangled her fingers in his dreads just as he reached her breast with his lips and then the unthinkable happened…the door opened and Talon walked in.

"Uhm excuse me, I must be in the wrong place because I know I'm not seeing what I think I'm seeing so I'ma go back out and try this shit again." He said turning around and walking out the door. Devah let her legs drop and tried to push Ra away but he wasn't having it. He buttoned her shirt back up and then lifted her off the counter but still held her in his arms.

"Ra! Oh my goodness! I can't believe Ta just walked in here and saw us." She said trying to get her composure and her breath back.

"So what? All we were doing was kissing, what's wrong with that?" Ra asked perplexed.

"Uhm, that was a whole lot more than a kiss Ra. And what's wrong? Hello we're in my place of business, anyone could have walked in here and saw that." She explained, "Ugh, I can't," she said shaking her head with her fingers on her forehead massaging her temples. "I…this is why you need a chaperone Ra, I can't be alone with you without losing my damn mind." She finished just as Talon walked back in.

"I walked all the way back to my car and back again only to discover I was in the right place to begin with. Ain't that some shit? So if I'm in the right place then you must be the wrong person. I mean you look like Devah but I don't know…" Talon said when he entered the store.

"Talon, not now. Puhleeze…not right now ok. I apologize for that but I…uhn uhn not now." She said throwing her hand up in the air and pleading with him to leave it alone…at least for now.

"Whateva Miss Diva, and I'm talking about the four letter word just so you know." He said with a smirk, Devah replied by giving him the finger.

"Hey Ra, what's up witcha?" he said walking over to give Ra a pound. "Besides your nature that is." He said before Ra could respond.

"Bruh, you got jokes huh?" Ra said laughing. "I'm just trying to get in some quality time, I gotta get in where I fit in with this one." He said looking at Devah.

Devah cut her eyes at both of them before storming off into her office. They watched as she walked away, mesmerized by the sway of her hips.

"If I didn't know you were married to a brick house beauty, I'd have already put out a hit on you the way you be watching my woman." Ra said never taking his eyes off of Devah.

"Bruh, I'm married NOT blind, that walk is a thing of beauty. But just to reassure you, I NEVER mix business with pleasure. I love Devah and I love working here, but more than that, I love and respect my WIFE and what we've built together and I wouldn't jeopardize that for nothing or no one a'ight? Look, why don't you get her outta here? Go have some fun, enjoy the day I got this."

Just then Devah came swinging back into the showroom.

"Thanks to you I can't concentrate," She said to Ra, "so we might as well get outta here and find something to do." She finished breezing past them and heading for the door.

"That was easier than I thought it'd be." Talon mumbled in surprise.

"Ta…zip it ok? You're not helping the situation none with your innuendos just so you know." She said stopping to glare at him.

"It's not an innuendo if it's the truth now is it?" Talon said before walking toward the back to put his things up not fazed at all by her 'mad' look. "Enjoy the rest of your day boss lady, Ra."

"For sure." Ra replied following behind Devah as she continued her march to the door.

"HELLO!" Shane said snapping her fingers bringing Devah back from her walk down memory lane.

"It was nice, actually it was great. We had a wonderful time but… I don't know; it's just all happening so fast. Like who falls like that, it's really fucked up when you can't trust your own feelings."

"Can't or won't Miss Devah?" asked Trena, one of the crew members who'd been with the family from the beginning and was not only a great masseuse but was also like family. Trena and her daughters owned their own spa in Summerville SC and one day Ri, Londa, Shane and Devah had been out shopping and decided to have an impromptu spa day and ran across Relax & Release Spa Treatments. Before they left the spa, Londa surprised everyone by asking Trena if she would like to work for them once they got the CAILIN up and running. Trena was honored but humbly declined as she couldn't afford to leave her business for months at a time without losing what clientele she did have. It was only her and her daughters and she didn't want to be away from them for long periods of time either. A week later Londa and Ri showed up at the spa with a group of ladies and a business plan that included her daughters and lots of traveling. Trena was so touched she had to walk away into her office so she wouldn't break down crying in front of everyone. Not knowing why she walked away the two walked into her space and found her on her knees giving God all the glory, thanks and praise for blessing her yet again. The two immediately joined her adding their praises to hers. They each wrapped an arm around her and held her as she thanked them over and over again, because she'd just found out that her rent was increasing and she was already at the top of her budget so she was going to have to close her doors. Ri immediately go up and called her husband, as this was one of the many buildings he'd worked on throughout the Carolinas she knew he knew who to call and what to do to work it all out for the good and that's just what he did. A month later Trena had the deed to her store and three trusted employees she and her daughters knew personally. She'd also had her lawyers draw up a contract that gave Londa & Ri ten percent apiece of her business leaving forty for herself and twenty each for her daughters. Londa and Ri declined and they all fussed and argued until they came to an impasse with Trena threatening to turn away their help and closing shop if they didn't accept and Ri and Londa compromising by taking only five percent apiece, after more arguing Trena finally agreed to their terms. Soon after they were all setting sail on the CAILIN when the yacht took its very first voyage.

"I don't know Tren."

"Miss Devah when all else fails pray. God gives every woman a great gift that we have to nurture and learn to trust."

"And what's this wonderful gift?" Three pairs of ears perked up to hear the answer to that question.

"It's called INTUITION." Trena answered sagely. "All done ladies, times up." She said as she and her daughters Trisa and Trika began clearing off their work space.

"Well damn, how come I didn't think of that?" Devah remarked drily.

"With age comes wisdom," Trena stated, "right nah yuh still young ahn dum'."

"Thanks a lot Tren." Devah said rolling her eyes while Lainy and Shane laughed.

"I don't know why those two ta laugh fuh." Tren admonished the ladies and falling into her native geechie language; she was born and raised on John Island in South Carolina.

"You, Miss Shane jus' had de love of yuh life propose to ya in a truly extravagant way ahn are on a cruise visiting some of de most romantic islands dere are ahn yet all day ahn every night yuh hanging out wit' dese four," she said including her daughters in her tirade, "instead of enjoying dis time wit' yuh fiancé. Ahn Miss Lainy, I don' know yuh dat well but yuh have got tuh be a special kind ah slow not tuh see 'ow much Mr. Shell loves yuh. Like I said…young ahn dumb." She finished shaking her head at the trio. "Go! All of dis nonsense is blocking my chi; I feel a headache coming on."

****

"On the real tho', I don't know what else to do." Shell addressed the men on the deck, "It's like she's scared or something."

"Or hiding something." said his uncle Zell, who'd dealt with some of the most scandalous hoes in the Chuck and didn't put nothing past a woman.

"Go 'head with that Uncle Zell, not every woman is like the broads you be dealing with. I know Lay loves me…"

"What's love got to do with it? Sheit, my women said they loved me too but they still been some dirty bitches."

"Zellis, that's enough with the bitches. Remember you're the one who keeps choosing those types of women so what does that make you son?" asked his father Ranauld 'Honey Bear' Actlin.

"That makes me SMART."

"How you figure Unc." asked Tre, the only one of the group without a significant other, at the moment anyway…by choice of course.

"Because I already know what I'm getting into, that way I know what's expected. Everybody plays their part, we have some fun, I spend some cash, get plenty of ass, well at least until they get tired of me cheating with their friends, sisters, cousins…"

"Don't forget the one whose mama you slept with!" laughed his brother Liq.

"Oh shit yeah, man Unc you was cold for that one right there." Stance said shaking his head at his uncle's escapades.

"Hey, how was I to know that was her mother sleeping in her bed? Shit I was three sheets to the wind and it ain't like she stopped me…she knew I wasn't her damn husband. Hell Ta'nya shouldn't've been telling her mother how good the dick was; her old lady just had to try it out for herself."

"So you tryna say you couldn't tell the difference between young pussy and old?" asked his oldest brother, Ranauld Jr. whom they all called BJ or Bear Jr. "You just the innocent party here huh bruh?"

"I ain't saying all of that, but I will say this...the difference between Ta'nya's pussy and her mama's is her mama's was wetter and way better! Old girl could throw down y'all bullshit if ya wanna! You could tell she wasn't used to getting good dick. Ooo Wee and let's not talk about that mouth of hers..."

"Damn ole girl been talking dirty too?" Tre asked.

"And when she finished, she sucked it clean with that same dirty mouth!" They all fell out laughing.

"Man Unc you hell!" said Gerauld, BJ's youngest son.

"Fo' sho cuz," Stance co-signed.

"Yeah but how does that story help me?" Shell wanted to know.

"It doesn't but it gotcha mind off your situation for a few didn't it neph?" replied Zell, causing everyone to laugh again.

"Aye man listen..." Ra began before Shell cut him off.

"Yo, on the real you can't tell me nothing 'cause you in the same boat I'm in bruh."

"And if he ain't, he better act like he is." Sean said, "I know you got more sense than to sit here and discuss anything that goes on with you and my daughter right son?"

"What? Y'all think I gotta death wish? All these Actlins surrounding me I would have to be crazy to do that." Ra replied with a smirk. "Man y'all don't scare me and just so y'all know this here ain't right. We all getting together to talk about what's going on in our various relationships, but I'm the only one who can't speak my mind without being threatened by my woman's family. Man that shit ain't right." Ra said shaking his head.

"Your woman huh? Feels good to say that and mean it don't it?" Sean teased Ra, "But on the real son, of course you can come to us if you need to talk, ain't nobody saying all that, it's just certain things we don't need to hear about you feel me?"

"If by that you mean sex…"

"Bingo…"

"I couldn't talk about that if I wanted to."

"Yeah, cause Devah would kill you." Tre said rubbing his throat.

"Naw that ain't it, that nigga ain't getting none!" Stance said tripping. "Didn't I warn your ass that same day we were planning this vacation? But naw bruh, you ain't wanna listen, now ya ass 'round here looking sick like this fool here." he finished nodding his head at Shell.

"Bruh, just because you finally gotcha girl, please don't make the mistake of thinking we forgot how sick you used to be worrying about what Shane and Devah were getting into, having niggas stalking every move she made to see who she was with and shit."

"Oh yeah," Jace piped in as CJ sat up. "Does Shane know the lengths you went to coerce her into this relationship?"

"Now wait one damn minute…"

"Naw grandpa, I got this one. The answer to your question Papa Jace…"

"Oh hell naw, *Papa Jace*? Boy you better off calling me uncle!" Jace said horrified at the name Stance had for him.

"Anyway," Stance said after he'd finished laughing, "to answer your question *pops*, and yours too big bruh...I saw how you sat up," he said addressing CJ, "I've been stalking her a helluva lot less than she has been me. I only saw her as a little sister when we were younger...it wasn't until later…when she got older and things started to change and develop, a whole lot I might add, that I started seeing her differently!" he said laughing some more.

"Ok the same rules that apply for Ra, apply for you Stance!" CJ interjected.

"'Bout damn time shit!" Ra said feeling better about things now that he wasn't the only one in the hot seat.

The group of men shared a good laugh before the eldest Actlin blessed them with some duly earned wisdom. "Listen," he addressed his grandson, "I've been around the playing field a few times back in the day and what I've learned is this," he said causing every ear to perk up with attention. "PATIENCE." he said and sat back in his lounger, crossed his ankles, pulled his shades down over his eyes and folded his arms over his chest.

"So dad you just gonna drop that one pearl of wisdom and then cut out on us? Come on old man I know you can do better than that." Tarik 'Rik' Actlin, his youngest son said.

"Nope, that's all I got for you fools today. But be sure to catch me tomorrow, I'll be here all week gents. Right now, I'm getting ready to catch up on my beauty sleep...besides with all of y'alls foolishness, I'm getting a headache." he said, dismissing the group.

"That's real foul pops."

"Yeah gramps."

"Fo' sho Mr. Bear."

They all grumbled as they left him to his rest.

"It ain't easy being me, but somebody gotta do it." was his response to all the complaints as he relaxed his 6'5, 310 pound frame of pure muscle, in the comfortable lounge chair.

Chapter 4

Jokes On Who

"Well, one down…"

"And too many more to go!" Ri finished Alonda's statement for her referring to Stance & Shane's engagement. "At least for me…you only have one more to go, I've got three." She said laughing.

"I don't know Ri, Shell & Devah might be down for the count sooner than you think. I'm just saying…" she added in response to the look her friend gave her.

"Girl please, Shell I can see," she stated nodding her head. "I really think he's feeling Lainy but for some reason she's holding back. I'm gonna sit down and have a talk with her when we get back to see where her head is at. But that damn daughter of mine? I'on know about all that, between her father, uncles, brothers and the two biggest culprits of all her damn grandfathers, she is spoiled rotten. Ain't nobody 'bout to put up with her for too long. I feel so bad for RaShiem 'cause that man doesn't know what he's getting himself into chasing after Devah like a little puppy."

"Honestly Ri, I don't see it like that."

"Like what, you don't really think he's interested in Devah?" Ri asked, perplexed.

"Oh no, I know he's interested in Devah, but I don't think he's chasing behind her, I think he's just making his presence known and allowing her to become comfortable before he goes in for the kill. I think he's getting his hunt on, and Devah's his prey. That is one sexy ass man, and he knows it too. Just like he knows that sooner or later he's gonna get Devah and when he does she won't know what hit her. Factor in what you said about her being spoiled and wow, let the fun begin because once he catches her he's gonna wish he never had!" Londa added laughing. "I can see him turning tail running in the opposite direction so fast it's not gonna be funny…or maybe it will be." She added and both women cracked up laughing again. "Poor thing, he's gonna have to learn the hard way."

"Who knows, maybe she's what he needs too…he's always so focused, intense you know. It's like he's still trying to prove he's not the person he used to be, always getting in trouble with the law, getting kicked out of school, one thing after another. I think it's high time that he left the past in the past and if anybody can get him outside of himself it would be Devah 'cause you know she ain't about to share the spotlight so his attention will *have* to be focused on her!" Ri stated, the two laughing hysterically now.

"Well it's nice to know I'm such a source of amusement for the two of you." Devah said standing in the doorway with her arms crossed.

"Devah!" Ri said turning around to face her daughter with a shocked expression on her face. Londa's look matched hers to a tee.

"Oh, don't stop on my account, I mean you two were going straight H.A.M. on me a few seconds ago, please…carry on. Let me know how you *REALLY* feel about me."

"Aww sweetie, we were just kidding around; you know we didn't mean anything by it. Don't be like that," Londa said walking towards Devah with her arms out for a hug.

"Naw, you can keep that auntie, I'm good." She said holding her right hand out like a big red stop sign, hurt showing clearly on her face and stopping Londa in her tracks.

"Devah, please don't blow things all out of proportion…"

"Yeah, 'cause that's the type of ish I'm known to do right Ma, after all I'm so spoiled and focused on myself, what else would I do but make it even more about me than it already is." Devah interrupted.

"Your aunt & I were just having a little fun…albeit at your expense. We're sorry honey, don't be mad." Her mother finished.

"Oh no, I'm not mad. It does my heart good to know how the two women I love, respect & admire the most think of me. I feel all warm & gooey inside." Devah replied sarcastically. "And to think, I was just coming to ask you guys for advice about Ra, but hell y'all just saved me the trouble…I know *exactly* how you feel. Thanks for making it crystal clear ladies, carry on." She said as she turned to walk out the door.

"Devah!"

"Dawnesha!" they yelled at her back as she rounded the corner.

"What the hell just happened?" Londa asked puzzled.

"I think we just stepped into the twilight zone." Ri answered.

"She has to know we were just tripping right? I mean she can't possibly be mad for real." She said shaking her head. "It's not like we were lying, her ass is spoiled," Londa said getting worked up over Devah's attitude. "And you know what…I'm gonna go find her & let her know I don't appreciate her funky ass attitude either!" she said headed for the door.

"No need, I'm right here." Devah said coming through the doorway with a grin on her face. "I was wondering how long it would take for you to get all worked up." She said addressing her aunt. "I got y'all good didn't I?" she asked laughing at the women who wore expressions similar to the ones they had when she walked in the room the first time.

"Bravo sis, I think that performance deserves a standing ovation, don't you all agree?" Shane said clapping as she and Lainy entered the room.

"I did that didn't I?" Devah said patting herself on the back before taking a bow.

"Wow, could you toot your own horn any louder?" Lainy said shaking her head at Devah.

"Wait a damn minute, you mean to tell me that little scene was all an act?" Londa asked in disbelief.

"You have got to be shitting me." Ri said looking ready to strangle her daughter.

"Lainy, if I could I would, auntie it sure was and Ma, I'm afraid not." Devah replied to the three of them.

"Ri, I'm 'bout to *really* go H.A.M. on your daughter, that heifer know she play too damn much."

"Yeah, well when you finish with her don't forget her cohorts." Ri said. "I'll help you get rid of the bodies." She added.

"You never did like getting your hands dirty." Londa replied.

"Reminds me of Shane." Devah said laughing. "It's funny how I'm most like you and Shane more like my mom."

"Uhn uh, don't try to change the subject, I'm gonna kick your little ass for that stunt…then I'm coming for the rest of you." Londa said looking at Shane and Lainy.

"No ma'am, I ain't have nothing to do with that." Lainy protested. "In fact I tried to talk both of them out of it, but they wouldn't listen to me…"

"You suck Lainy, we s'pose to be in this together, how you gonna do us like that?" Shane asked.

"Look, I'm not about to get my ass kicked by your mom. If you're so down then take my ass cuttin' for me. The only time I actually liked getting spanked was the only time I had sex and that was…oh shit," Lainy said covering her mouth and catching herself before finishing her sentence and calling Shell's name. "My bad, I didn't mean to take it that far."

"Too late now…so you like getting spanked when you getcha freak on huh?" Devah asked, with a dimpled smile and a raised brow.

"No she 'liked' getting spanked, as in past tense, the *only* time she 'had sex and that was '…when and with whom? And why aren't you still having sex with this dude if you liked it so much? And it's very obvious that you did so don't bother denying it. And when you say 'only' you don't actually mean that's the only time you've had sex do you?" Shane paused, eyeing Lainy's figure then shook her head, "No, that can't be what you meant. Does Shell know about this? If he has some competition I think he should know don't you?" She questioned.

"Damn, you finished?" Lainy asked.

"And patiently waiting for answers I might add." Came the flip reply.

"Well the answer to all your questions and yours too Devah is none ya, as in none of your business, y'all just nosy as hell. I know you guys are real comfortable discussing your private business, in detail I might add, amongst one another and sometimes others and that's cool but I'm not, so this conversation will not be happening. Ma, auntie," as she'd taken to calling Ri and Londa, "I apologize for my crassness, I think your daughters are starting to rub off on me." She said embarrassed.

"Lainer please, you are far from being little Miss Innocent ok?" Ri responded waving her hand at Lainy.

"For real." Londa co-signed. "If you're hanging with these two than you're already guilty by association."

"Thanks a lot Mom."

"You're welcome sweetie."

"I-Wha-huh?" Lainy stuttered trying to get a word in.

"But back to the topic," Devah cut her off again, "Shane I think you were on to something. What was it she said just now…' The only time I actually liked getting spanked was the only time I had sex and that was…', did I get it right?" she asked the others, leaving Lainy out of the equation.

"Yeah, I think that's about right." Ri responded.

"Sooo, the way you cut the rest of your sentence off, that could only mean one thing…" Devah paused for effect, "you were talking about…"

"Dawnesha Devah Actlin…don't you dare finish that sentence!" Lainy cut her off, horrified. "Oh my goodness, are you serious? I don't believe this, how did I get on the hot seat? I thought this was about you and Shane getting spanked…not me. Can we please just change the subject?" she said, face on fire.

"Hey you opened the door; all we did was step through." Shane said shrugging her shoulders. "Don't get mad at us for your faux pas." She finished, eyebrow raised and arms crossed.

"The hand of one is the hand of all…at least that's what the law says." Londa replied, "As far as I'm concerned you're just as guilty as these two for that little prank. With that being said I believe the topic of spanking is very much open, what do you guys think? And since you don't want me to tarnish the memory of your previous 'spanking' I say the least you could do is quench our curiosities. All in favor of Devah finishing that statement say aye."

"AYE!" four sets of voices yelled in unison.

"NAY!" said Lainy. "Devah puh-leeeze do NOT finish that statement. Please don't put my business out there like that because I promise you I'll be on the next thing smoking, headed back home if you do." Lainy said seriously.

"Whoa, it's like that Lainy?" Londa asked.

"Yes auntie…it is."

"You got that Lainy, I'mma keep it to myself," Devah said with an impish grin, "but you know you're family too right? We don't judge one another and we keep it one hunnid at all times, what's said between us stays between us ok? You don't have to share everything...yet," she added side eyeing Lainy, "but you also don't have to be afraid *to* share either." Devah said.

"Duly noted." She responded quickly.

"Ok y'all, let's leave Lainy alone. Devah you said you came in here to talk to me and your aunt about Ra, right?"

"Yes." Devah answered.

Lainy breathed a sigh of relief, glad to finally be off of the hot seat but not missing the thoughtful look Ri was giving her from across the room. She'd heard when Ri said she would have a talk with her when they got back home and she planned to avoid the grandmother of her children as long as she could.

Chapter 5

Some Gets Some...

As the women came back on board after an evening of sightseeing and bar hopping, they found their men playing cards and shooting pool in the lounge area. "Oh my goodness, we'll never get them outta here. They've already settled in and gotten comfortable." Anesha Actlin sighed, shaking her head at her husband, offspring and all of their cohorts.

"We should've never left them alone." Replied her daughter-in-law.

"There go my plans for relaxing." Londa muttered.

"Mom, shouldn't this be the time for you to relax while daddy is here with the guys and no one is there to disturb you?" Shane asked.

"That goes to show just how much you know. You and I obviously have two very different ideas of relaxation lil girl. Your father is the reason I'm always so relaxed sweetie." Londa told her horrified daughter.

"Ma!!! TMI…entirely too much!" Shane stated before heading towards the bar for something to erase the image of her parents 'relaxing' from her mind.

"Why ask a question if you don't want to know the answer? Everyone relaxes differently and it's not like I don't have other forms of relaxation, I was just looking forward to…"

"Auntie, for real for real, it sounds like we're about to have another TMI moment here so please, stop while you're ahead." Devah advised.

"Oh forget you two, y'all are just jealous."

"Uh yeah, because I'm as head over heels in lust with uncle Jace as you are with my man right? Lady get a grip ok?"

"Auntie, you got a little crush on me?" Ra asked, walking up on the ladies from behind, winking at her and causing Londa to blush. Reaching out he pulled Devah into his arms, "because I know you were referring to me when you said your man right?" he asked before bending down to give her a kiss. Ri and Londa shared a knowing look.

"Maybe…maybe not." Came the saucy reply.

"Yeah, whatever…whether you wanna admit it or not, this right here is a done deal. Ain't no backsies," he said causing Devah to laugh, "we in this for the long haul. I ain't going no where and neither are you."

"Well damn, do I get a say in this decision?" Devah asked sarcastically.

"Yes."

"Well thanks a lot; it's good to know I have a choice."

"No, I meant 'yes' as in that's your say in this decision, not yes as in you have a choice." Ra said laughing as Devah tried unsuccessfully to pull away from him. "Trust me, I got you." He said looking in her eyes, all signs of joking completely gone leaving nothing but the truth of his intentions and convictions. Just like that all of the fight left Devah as she nodded once and relaxed against him.

"Oh my goodness! You're just as conceited as your father." Kezzie said looking at her son and shaking her head.

"But not as bullheaded." He responded before leaning over to giving her a kiss on the cheek. "How'd you enjoy the island?"

"I beg to differ and you do know this isn't the first time I've been to Martinique right? Your father and I have been here a few times before."

"Yeah but look who you said you were here with. I've been on many vacations with you guys and every time it's the same routine. Hit every tourist trap there is in the time we have available. He never goes outside of the guidelines established by the travel brochures, the concierge or the hotel staff…boring. At least with these adventure seekers, I know you got to see parts of the island you didn't even know existed. Not to mention the shopping and the restaurants, in other words…not boring." Ra said smiling at his mom to cut the sting of his words.

"Honey that's what you remember, but son trust me when I tell you that when you guys were in for the night with the hotel sitter service, your father and I had many an illicit adventure. If only you knew…"

"Mom, I don't really think I want to know, thanks."

"Yes, please stop her before she embarrasses you like my mom did." Shane said having rejoined the group with something fruity and alcoholic in her hand.

"Anyway, Von just wanted you two to enjoy yourselves and that's why he made sure you guys got to do all the things that were advertised in those brochures, he wanted you to have fun…not be bored."

"I'm sorry ma, I didn't mean to make it sound as if I didn't enjoy our vacations, because I did. I was thinking of you when I said it must have been boring, watching us do all of those thrill seeking, adventurous things while you sat on the sidelines cheering us on."

"Yeah, 'cause I'm nobody's fool! I wasn't doing all those crazy things the three of you found to do. I was fine watching from a distance, watching you guys was good enough for me, I didn't actually have to experience it. I lived vicariously through the three of you."

"You ain't slick Mrs. Kezzie, I done peeped your game. You just waited 'til later to have your fun." Lainy said laughing.

"And plenty of it too I might add." She said with a raised eyebrow, "In that respect I totally agree with Londa, my husband is the reason I keep a smile on my face and pep in my step." She finished, shocking her son into silence as he promptly buried his face in the curve of Devah's neck and covered his ears.

"That's what I'm talkin' about, preach Kezzie!" Londa exclaimed. "Y'all gon' learn today!" she said laughing.

"Alright, alright, alright!" Ri joined in on the fun.

"Uhn uh…pine APPLES! No more Kevin Hart for either of you." Devah told them shaking her head.

"Actually I like plums better." Ri said.

"Peaches for me." Replied Kezzie.

"Pie." Said Anesha with a smile.

"Well mine would be pu…"

"Auntie!"

"Ma!"

"Yo!"

"What? What's wrong with puddin'?" Londa asked with a devious smile.

"You had me worried for a minute too." Ri said. "I didn't know what was getting ready to come out of that raunchy mouth of yours."

"You know I gotta keep y'all on your toes. But anywho, back to the subject at hand…how the hell am I gonna get Jace off that pool table short of walkin' through this joint in my birthday suit?"

"I am so outta here." Shane said with a look of disbelief on her face as she looked at her mom before walking over to her father and whispering in his ear. Jace looked up at his wife, slowly undressed her with his eyes, licked his lips, put his pool stick down, and grabbed his money amidst protests and jeers from the other men. Never taking his eyes of Londa, he walked over, grabbed her hand and headed toward the exit.

Londa looked back at the group with a huge smile and winked her eye. She then blew a kiss to her daughter who rolled her eyes and shook her head at her parents.

"Tomorrow can't get here quick enough for me." Kezzie said wistfully. "I'm in dire need of a fix."

"That's my cue to leave. Devah, don't make any plans, I got a few things up my sleeve for tonight."

"You're wearing a tank top…you don't have any sleeves. You must not have much planned." She said eyeing his muscled arms, chest, thighs…whew.

"You got jokes huh?" he nodded his head, licking his lips, "Just be ready by 9 a'ight? Wear something sexy, we doing it big." he said eyeing her back, his eyes filled with sensual promises of an unforgettable night, before heading back over to finish playing cards…all eyes on him.

"I must say…he gets that swagger from his daddy!" Kezzie said breaking the trance the other women were under, causing everyone to laugh except for Devah. All of a sudden she didn't feel too well…her stomach was hurting.

"Shane what did you say to your father to get him to leave like that. Especially since he was running the table, we all know Jace don't walk away from free money, you must have said something real interesting to get him to leave."

"I told him what he needed to hear."

"Which was…?"

"Wouldn't you like to know?" Shane teased Ri. "I guess us young'uns aren't the only ones who gon' learn today!" she said laughing.

"Forget you Shane, and whatever it is you said to your father, go tell your uncle. I find myself in need of some 'relaxation' too." Ri said eyeing Sean like a predator.

"No can do, that's what you got Devah for, my job is done for tonight. The only other man I'm working on now is mine and believe me, I know exactly how to get him up off that table. Watch and learn ladies." She said walking over to Stance. She ran her nails across the back of his neck, ending with her index finger under his chin, turning his head toward her and looking in his eyes before sauntering off towards the exit with a seductive twist in her hips, where she paused lifting that same index finger and beckoning him with it, never once looking back to see if he was looking or if he would follow her…that was a given as far as she was concerned. Stance stared at the empty doorway for a few seconds, wiped his mouth, shook his head, threw in his hand and got up from the table.

"I fold." He said, ignoring the men as he hurried after his fiancé, who was holding the elevator for him.

"That must be some helluva, helluva." Zell said picking up the hand Stance had thrown in. "That fool just folded with a royal flush! He was about to take all of our asses to the cleaners." He chuckled, thanking Shane for her timing and her libido.

"And here I thought he was bluffing, I was about to call his ass." Liq said relived too with Shane's timing.

"I still can't figure out if he knows what he's doing or if he's just one lucky motherfucker. Just when you think he's down and out…BOOM," BJ said, opening his closed fist like a bomb blowing up, "he hits you with a hand like this." He pointed at the cards now laying face up on the table. "I just don't know." He finished shaking his head.

"And therein lies the crux of the situation," Ra said indicating the table at large, "you all don't know…but I do." He laughed as he stood up from the table. "Which is why I know when to hold 'em and when to fold 'em."

"Well shit you just told us all we gotta do from now on is to follow your lead." Said Zell.

"Or…I just set you up for the kill." Ra smirked, "Gentlemen it's been real but I've got a hot…and I do mean hot, date tonight with a beautiful young lady so I have to go get my grown man on. I'mma holla at you all tomorrow…good night and God bless."

"Hey neph,"Zell called out to Ra, "don't do anything I would do." He said in all seriousness, he and his brothers mean mugging Ra.

"Well that doesn't leave much now does it unc?" Ra responded.

"Exactly."

"Yeah well I'll tell you what, I won't go no further than I'm allowed…a'ight?" he grinned walking off ignoring the veiled threats issued by Devah's uncles. He was on a mission and his mission was to please.

51

Chapter 6

Some Gets None ...

Qua watched Lainy as she mingled with the enemy, which is what he'd come to think of anyone associated with Shellon Actlin. When he'd heard Devah urging Lainy to go on vacation with her family he knew Shell had put her up to it. At first Lainy had been adamant about not going but eventually that bitch Devah had worn her down. Again his ear hustling had paid off in a major way and there was no way in hell he was letting Lainy go anywhere with Shell without him being there to block his opponent…in any way he could. He got to work hacking into the CAILIN'S computer system and seeing where he could find a fit for himself. After tampering with some of the inventory and making it seem as if things were disappearing from the kitchen, management was called to task and eventually a few of the staff were let go. Feeling no remorse for costing anyone their jobs, Qua quickly placed himself in a position to get to know different members of the crew and get plugged in with those who had authority. After inhabiting the after hour spots and different water holes the crew hung out at and establishing solid relationships with those who could further aid his cause he went in for the kill. He started dropping hints that he was looking for a new job, mentioning that he was a sous chef but that he'd been thinking of quitting because he wanted to travel the world and experience different cultures. The head cook then mentioned that the yacht he worked on was looking for a cook and would be sailing to St. Lucia for the Christmas holiday. He told Qua he should apply for the job to which he promptly complied after forging some phony credentials and references to get hired on. It's a good thing he covered all his bases because Sean and Jace had thoroughly checked him out, and even though they were still waiting for some of his bogus paperwork to clear they hired him on because they didn't have any other prospects…he'd made sure of that too. He'd not only created a new identity, but also a new look. He was sure that no one who knew him would recognize him, but he stayed clear of them all the same just to be on the safe side. As he stood in the hallway watching Lainy, he saw Shell walk up to her and hug her from behind. He immediately saw red and probably would have blown his cover if another one of the cooks hadn't picked just that moment to stand beside him.

"They be getting it in up in there my nig!" he said to Qua, who was now using the alias Quin, short for Quince, since it still had the Que sound and it wouldn't be that much of a change to remember.

"Looks like it." he responded drily, not taking his eyes off of Lainy and Shell. He noticed Shell whisper something in Lainy's ear; she blushed and tilted her head back into his shoulder to give him a kiss and then ducked her head back down shyly. Shell placed his finger under her chin and lifted her head up for a more intimate and thorough kiss, heating Qua's blood to past boiling.

"Yo Q, you alright man? You look like you 'bout ready to blow a gasket bruh." Smiley said, something is off with this dude he thought to himself.

"I'm good, don't worry about me, my mind was somewhere else. Believe me, I got everything under control, I'm 'bout to make shit happen." Qua said walking away from his co-worker. "And for future reference my name is Quin, not Q bruh."

"Shit half the time we got to call you 2 or 3 times before you even answer so I figured Q would work better, but whatever dude. Maybe you should try answering to your name sometime." Smiley said to Qua's retreating back, no longer smiling.

"Problems Smiley?" Tre asked walking up on the last part of the conversation.

"Naw Tre, just one of the new guys acting weird. I don't know but something about that dude rubs me the wrong way." Smiley said to his best friend since kindergarten.

"How so? Has he done or said something out of the way, do I need to talk to Pop and Unc about him?"

"Not yet bruh, but I'ma keep my eye on him. You already know what it is; once my antenna goes up I can't leave it alone until I find out why. I'ma call this in and have someone run a trace on him."

"Pop and Jace already did that bruh."

"Yeah, but they don't have the resources I have at my disposal. I'll have my team get on it right away."

"Hey, you're the best…"

"That I am." Smiley boasted, cutting Tre off.

"Yeah a'ight, you finished patting ya back big head?" Tre responded shaking his head at him. "Anyway, that's why we hired you to begin with. With this crazy shit that has been going on with our computers and not being able to pinpoint where it's coming from, a lot of the people who work for us are suspect. Anyway bruh, since you're here, how 'bout you get back on your other J-O-B and bring me some wings to eat?" Tre laughed at the look on Smiley's face.

"Don't push it bruh, for real yo. You gon' mess 'round and have a real upset stomach fuckin' with me." Smiley said walking away with a smirk on his face at the look that was now on Tre's.

"Aye yo Smiley, seriously don't play like that. It's in your job description bruh!" He said to Smiley's disappearing back. "You know you make some mean wings, why you trippin' bruh?" he yelled after him laughing. Tre looked at his phone that was vibrating &

ringing in his hand; he didn't recognize the number but he had a pretty good idea who it was so he answered anyway.

"Hello?"

"Hey, enjoying your vacation?" the person on the other end asked.

"Yes, very much so. Who's this?" he asked, knowing he was getting under her skin.

"Give outcha number a lot huh?"

"Mostly for business purposes, but every now and again…on a personal basis. Which one is this?"

"Definitely the latter, but since you can't seem to remember who you gave your number to, then I'ma let you go boo. Enjoy the rest of your vacay a'ight?"

"Aye yo Zi, don't play baby girl." Tre said before she could hang up.

"Ohhh now you know who I am? What gave me away?"

"It was probably that 'I don't give a fuck' attitude you seem to have down pat. But really…I'd know that voice anywhere, I just wanted to see how long it would take before you let that temper loose." He said grinning into the phone.

"Yeah right, whatever Tre. You *play* too much you know…I swear I don't know whether or not to take you serious. That's why I can't be fucking with you like this, I swear you'll make me hurt you for real dude, I just can't deal." Zi said wiping all laughter from Tre's voice as he responded.

"Baby girl, why we gotta keep going through this shit? You already know what it's hitting for with me. You're the one who keeps running, not me so g'on with that bullshit you talking. I'ont care *how* much I play, when it comes to you on some real g shit...I'm dead dog serious, I ain't playing no games...yo what the fuck is you laughing for Zi? I'm serious right now."

"Yeah I know..." she said between laughter, "dead dog serious at that!" Zi said falling out again. "Really Tre? You couldn't come up with anything better than that? Oh my gosh, that shit there is too damn funny...dead dog serious." Zi repeated cracking up on the other end.

"Now who's playing too much?" Tre asked shaking his head and finally cracking a grin at Zi trippin' on the phone. "How 'bout you call me back when you're finished. This is technically an overseas call you know and although I love the sound of your laughter I'd rather hear it in person."

"Aww that's so sweet Tre but nevertheless, I don't see that happening anytime soon so…"

"I do, why don't you join us for the last week of our vacation?"

"Uh, 'cause my money is funny and I can't just pop-up on your family's vacation trip. What would they think if I did some shit like that? Uhn uhn, *not* happening boo boo."

"They would think that you were here for me, which you would be, besides you were invited and as far as getting here don't worry about all that, I got it."

"The hell you do, that's alright, I'm good. You go 'head and enjoy the rest of your trip, just holla at me when you get home…so you better make sure you lock my number in because the next time we talk, you'll be the one calling." She said.

"You already know it's automatic that I'ma lock ya number in but peep this…you'll be seeing me a lot sooner than you think a'ight? 'Til then…be good baby girl, one." Tre said ending the call and searching out his father.

Chapter 7

This Ain't No Game

"Bae, you got my dick harder than a ma'fucka." Shell whispered in Lainy's ear as he kissed alongside her neck making her nipples so tight they were hurting and her bra wasn't helping any, she wanted to whip it off and strangle Shell with it.

"Shell stop, people can see you y'know." She said looking around to see if anyone was watching them.

"Fuck them, they'll be a'ight. Damn your nipples so big and hard right now I wanna suck them joints so bad." He groaned brushing his fingers across her right nipple causing her to moan and shudder as an ache spread from her nipples down to her stomach and then through her lower regions causing her to close her eyes, arch her back and press back into him forgetting about everyone else in the room. All that mattered was what Shell had been saying and doing to her for the past hour, teasing her body and feeding her imagination until she was ready to...

"Shell," Lainy said breathlessly.

"Yeah Bae?"

"Let's go to your room." She said.

"Naw Lainy, I ain't tryna be walking 'round here with blue balls 'cause you wanna play with me."

"Ain't nobody playing. You coming or not?" she asked, walking towards the exit.

Shell grabbed Lainy's arm before she'd gone three steps and pulled her back to face him. What he saw in her eyes confirmed what he was thinking but he wanted, no he needed more than that, he had to have verbal confirmation as well.

"Lainy just so we're clear and there's no misunderstanding; let me get something straight with you before we do this. If we go to my room…ain't no turning back, it's going down. *All* night and well into the next day too. Any and *every* way I can get you…are we clear?"

"Crystal." She said before heading toward the exit. Shell watched her for a few seconds, not believing she was going to finally let him make love to her again. Shell adjusted himself in his pants and pulled his shirt down to hide his massive erection, then he headed out after Lainy.

"Shell," Ri said having watched them the whole time on the low. She knew Lainy had been holding out on Shell and that he'd been real patient with her, showing her with his actions that he meant everything he'd said to her and not pushing her and she was real proud of him for manning up like that. But she could see as clear as day that things had just been turned up a notch and she wanted to make sure Shell was thinking with a clear head, or more to the point…with the head on his shoulders.

"Ma, can this wait 'til tomorrow? I'm kinda in a rush."

"Yes, I can see that which is exactly why you need to slow down before you go into overdrive son."

"Ma, what are you talking about?" Shell said looking up at the exit wanting to catch up with Lainy, praying she wasn't going to change her mind.

"You and Lainy. I can see the handwriting on the wall and I know what's about to go down…"

"You have got to be freakin' kiddin' me," Shell said looking at his mother horrified. "Are you tryna talk to me about the birds and the bees Ma, 'cause if so dad already covered this subject like 15 years ago." He said in a low voice. "This ain't my first rodeo show, I've been around the track a few times already Ma." He joked.

"Boy ain't nobody talking about no damn birds, bees or rodeo shows for that matter, I'm talking about YOU and Lainy. I just want you to take ya time son, because even though *you've* been around the track a few times, as mature as Lainy may be I don't think she has, so please slow your roll and take ya damn time. That's all I wanted to say ok? Go…enjoy your night but even more so make sure *she* enjoys it." She advised her son.

"A'ight Ma, I hear you, but on the real I got this. I've waited to damn long to get ba…" Shell caught himself, "to screw it all up now." He said turning to head for the door but bumping into his father instead. He really hoped they hadn't caught his slip. Lainy would kill him if she thought they knew about them *before* as opposed to now.

"Before you head in for the night," Sean said clearing his throat and raising one eyebrow, hands in his pockets, "why don't you head on down to the pharmacy first so you can make sure you're well prepared for any, uh extracurricular activities." He

59

said looking Shell in the eye. "We wouldn't want any ah, unplanned circumstances to occur."

"Well if anyone knows about unplanned circumstances, it's certainly you two." Shell said teasing his parents about Stance's birth. "But don't worry, I got enough to last for a month and I'm trying to use about half of them between tonight and tomorrow so if you'll excuse me...I got some work to put in." He said once again heading for the exit and this time making it.

"Oh my...I feel for that poor girl, Shell is gonna wear her out. She'll be lucky if he lets her come up for air or get some rest in between rounds."

"You sitting her all worried about her, but who's worrying about what I'm 'bout to do to you?" Sean said lustfully.

"Baaaby, you ain't said a thang, I been waiting for you since I got back on this yacht. Huh, you better hope *your* ass can walk when I finish with you mister." Ri retorted, gathering the things she'd bought and handing them to her husband. "Let's do this." He said.

"Yes, let's," she agreed.

"You know you've just awakened the beast with all that trash talk right?"

"Who do you think I was talking to when I said it?" she replied, sauntering toward the elevator.

"Mmh, I'ma tear that pussy up!" he mumbled as he followed behind Ri.

Chapter 8

Let's Ride

Ra knocked on Devah's door at nine on the dot. He almost drooled when he saw what she was wearing. Devah had on a short, tangerine colored halter dress that stopped just above her knees and when he looked down he noticed the metallic gold fuck me heels she had on. She accessorized her outfit with gold bangles on one arm and on the other a wide gold cuff linked by a chain to a large gold cuff ring on her middle finger, gold hoop earrings and a triple strand gold chain necklace all which she'd designed and made herself.

"Yo…why you wanna do this to me? How in the hell am I supposed to make it through the night with you wearing that?" he asked.

"What? You don't like it." Devah asked with a devilish grin.

"I like it too damn much, that's the problem." He replied.

"Good because I wore it just for you." She said wrapping her arms around his neck and giving him a kiss. "Ooh, at least somebody's happy to see me." She smirked referring to his hard-on.

"Yeah, that's the problem…he's a little too happy. The night is just getting started and from the looks of things he's gonna be like this all damn…what the fuck?" Ra said turning Devah around so he could see the back of her dress confirming with his eyes what his hands already knew. "Yo, Ma where is the rest of your damn dress?" he said staring at her bare backed halter dress, which left very little to the imagination, stopping just before the top of her very ample ass, "Some shit missing in'it?" he asked.

"Really Ra, I'ma need for you to gather ok? This dress covers everything that needs to be covered so quitcha bitchin' and let's ride out." She said reaching down to get her purse.

"YO! Why you look like you ain't got no draws on Ma? What you got going on?"

"First of all I rarely wear any type of underwear, only when necessary if you know what I mean." She said referring to her monthly. "Second, I don't EVER wear draws, period. Panties, thongs, g-strings, boy shorts for the most part but draws… uhn uhn boo. And finally to answer your question, I don't have anything going on, I am wearing a pair of thongs and that's only because I have no choice when I'm around you! Now let's go."

"Uhn uhn, not so fast Shorty, whatchu mean by that last comment? Why you only put on draws…my bad, underwear when you 'round me? What…that's supposed to protect you or something, 'cause if so I can tell you right now that shit ain't gonna work Ma."

"Not to protect me but to protect my clothes. Now come on, you said we had reservations for 9:45, it's ten after now."

"Your clothes…what in the hell is that supposed to mean?"

"Oh my gosh," Devah said exasperated, "Ra remember that day at Stance's house when I was walking up the stairs and you very rudely pointed out that the back of my…"

"Ohhh, I get it now." He said laughing. "Daaamn, it's like that and you ain't even get the D yet? Ma, you gon' be in troubleeee." He said, shaking his head and then laughing when Devah hit him with her gold evening clutch.

"Ooohh, you get on my freakin' nerves sometimes." She said sashaying out the door, her ass dancing up and down like a plate of jello in her short dress. "And stop looking at my ass!" she said feeling his eyes burning a hole through her dress and soaking her liner. Good thing she bought some extras with her…she was gonna need them. Ra laughed out loud as he closed her door behind him. As he took a step to follow her he remembered his own predicament and realized it was gonna be a very long and uncomfortable night thinking of ways to get Devah out of that dress and into his bed.

****

Shell entered his room hoping that Lainy was there waiting for him, hopefully naked and spread out in the middle of his bed.

"Lay?" he said walking into the sitting room and heading for the bedroom when he didn't see her sitting in there. He walked in his room and it too was empty.

"Damn!" he exclaimed, turning around to go back out and find Lainy.

"It took you forever to get here so I went ahead and took a shower...I hope that's not a problem." Lainy said from behind him. Shell turned back and saw Lainy coming out of the bathroom wrapped in a towel, her chocolate hued skin glistening wet and all he could think of was licking her dry and then making her wet all over again.

"Not at all, but if you'd waited it could have been a whole lot more fun with me in it." He said licking his lips.

"I'm sure there'll be other times when we can have fun taking a shower together, but right now all I want is for you to do all of those nasty, freaky things you've been whispering in my ear for the last few hours...no, make that months. Do you think you can do that?" she asked him.

"No doubt, you sure you're ready for this? I got a lot to let off my chest." He smirked.

"*You*...Shell I haven't had sex since the last time we did this. I really hope it's as good as I remember." She teased.

"Oh wow, you doubting my skills Bae? I guess I'm just gonna have to show and prove. But don't say I didn't warn you." He said coming up out of his clothes, headed in her direction.

"Duly noted." She said dropping her towel and standing there in all her glory.

"Damn Bae, I don't know how long this first round is gonna last because I'm ready to bust right freakin' now just from looking at you. But I promise I'll spend the rest of the night making up for it." He said reaching for Lainy, rubbing his hands over her body, reacquainting himself with the feel of her in his hands, the heft of her breast, the curve of her ass.

"I want your lips on me…now." Shell said looking in Lainy's eyes. She wrapped her arms around his neck and did as she was told, coming out of her box and letting all of her inhibitions go she kissed Shell with a passion so fiery hot he burned for more.

"Bae I can't wait, please don't be mad a'ight? I got to have you now or I'ma bust." He whispered hotly in her ear, trembling in her arms.

"I think it's hot that you want me so bad, why would I be mad about that?" she said reaching down and enclosing his straining erection in her hand. He was so thick she couldn't close her fingers around it so she used her other hand too.

"Ssss, damn Bae you tryna unman me or something?" he said grabbing for her wrists to still her hands. He put her arms back around his neck and lifted her up, sitting her down on the tip of his dick. Lainy tensed up when she felt him at her entrance stretching her wide.

"Lainy…I swear I'm 'bout a jackass for asking you this, but do you want me to stop?" he said, stopping himself from going any further with herculean effort.

"No, I'm sorry. I'm just a little scared…it's a lot bigger than I remembered and I'm scared it's gonna hurt." She admitted. "I had to have been hella drunk that first time to have let you put that in me." She said looking down at his penis. "No wonder I was so sore afterwards, had me walking funny for a whole damn week!"

"Did you enjoy yourself?"

"You know I did."

"Then that's all that matters isn't it?" Shell replied before nibbling on her bottom lip. "And before the night is over, you're gonna enjoy yourself all over again. Whatever pain you may feel won't be nothing compared to the pleasure you're about to receive a'ight?" Lainy nodded her head.

Shell walked over to the bed and laid her across it then dropped to his knees, spread her legs, opened up her vaginal lips and buried his face in it, sucking, and nibbling on her clit and licking her like a lollipop. Shell inserted one finger than two, loosening her up and getting her ready for his entrance.

"Oooh Shell, ohhh that feels so damn good baby, please don't stop." Lainy moaned holding his head, squeezing her thighs together and riding his face and fingers forgetting about his size, just wanting him in her. Shell started licking her from her opening to her clit with long broad strokes and she started losing it, clutching the sheets and bucking up off the bed.
"Ohhh shit, th-that feels sooooo go-goood." She stuttered. "Shell I-I think I'mma…oooh shit, I'm 'bout to cuummm." She moaned as she released her essence into his waiting mouth. Shell lapped up her juices adding another finger to the mix readying her even more as he used his other hand to guide himself into her. Lainy was so far gone she couldn't think straight, her body weakened from her tumultuous orgasm. When Shell pushed into her, she tensed from the painful burning sensation, grabbing his forearms and holding her breath.

"Relax Bae, I'm not gonna hurt you. I got you…breathe." He said as he pushed forward, stretching her walls 'til he was nuts deep in her. He stilled himself, letting her get used to his girth and her body being opened up again. Damn she was tight, she felt like a virgin gripped 'round his dick. He leaned down and kissed her.

"You a'ight?"

"Yeah, I'm good."

"You think you ready for the real thing now?" he asked biting on his bottom lip.

"You look so sexy when you do that Shell. You be making my pussy so wet when you bite on your lip like that."

"Lay," he groaned, "yo I'm trying not to bust right now but if you keep talking like that it's gonna be over before it even begins." He warned her.

"Then I guess you'll have to make it up to me for the rest of the night…won't you?"

"Fuck," Shell said, no longer able to stay still in her wet, hot heat. "Let me know if I hurt you Bae." He said moving slowly in and out of Lainy with long, deep strokes, feeding her his dick like it was part of a buffet. "Lay, your pussy feels so damn good. That shit so hot and wet…" he whispered in her ear making her so wet her pussy started making loud squishy noises. "So fucking good…uhm. Ssss, you so tight Lay, uhm I'm trying not to cum Bae." He groaned almost losing it when Lainy caught his rhythm and started moving with him. "Aaahhh Bae, oh shit ooooh I…ooooh"

"Don't hold back Baby get yours…," she said before remembering a vital piece of information…this was exactly how she got pregnant the last time they had sex, "Oh shit! Shell pull out!"

"What?"

"You didn't put on a condom and I'm not tryna have anymo…any kids right now! Damn," she said as she felt Shell release some of his hot jism in her even as he pulled out.

"Bae…my bad. Damn, I got caught up in the moment and forgot all about using a condom." He shook his head and chuckled.

"Shell please tell me what's so damn funny, 'cause I could really use a good laugh right now." She said thinking of the repercussions of their actions.

Shell rolled off Lainy and pulled her in his arms.

"Would you believe my parents just gave me the grown up version of the birds and the bees and my father actually suggested that I head to the pharmacy so I'd be prepared for any 'extracurricular activities' and avoid any 'unplanned circumstances'." He said. "I told him I had enough condoms for a month and then turned around and didn't even use one."

"Shell, please tell me you're just joking and you and your parents were not discussing the two of us having sex…PLEEEAAASE!" She said dismayed.

"Well *I* didn't…not really, but…Lainy come on, Ma stopped me before I could get out of the door and just when I thought I was done with her, I bumped into Pops. That's what took me so long, Bae what was I supposed to do? It's not like they don't know where together Lay."

"Come again…I'm here as Devah's friend, not your girlfriend, woman or whatever you want to call it."

"Lainy, let's be real here. A blind man can see how much I love and care for you, and I don't care how much you try to fight it you feeling me the same way too so yeah you're mine so you can kill that extra shit you talking. And Devah may have been the one who convinced you to come but that's only 'cause you kept turning me down for crazy ass reasons. You couldn't use those same excuses with Devah, because she's not interested in you in a physical way, but you beat me over the head with them." He said laughing at her look of outrage.

"Crazy excuses? I don't think so, my reasons were very clear and valid…not to mention justified. Annnddd furthermore, I was right."

"How so?"

"Did we not just get finish doing what I was afraid we'd end up doing?"

"Did you not *ask* to come to my room knowing what would happen if you did? Lay it was gonna happen eventually anyway; I don't see what the problem is. Didn't you enjoy all fifteen minutes of it?" he joked.

"Screw you Shell." She said trying not to laugh with him. He grabbed her by her waist and lifted her in the air bringing her body across his so she was straddling him. Then he reached in his nightstand and grabbed a condom handing it to her.

"What do you want me to do with this?"

"You just said you wanted to screw me, this time I'm making sure we cover all our bases." He smirked.

"You better hope we didn't hit a damn homerun that first time." She countered, like we did the last time she thought to herself.

"I would love to see you glowing and growing with my seed...one day." He told her.

"Really?"

"Yeah, Lainy I don't know why you keep doubting me, but I'm telling you now...I ain't going nowhere. Besides from what I've heard pregnant pussy is the best." He said laughing as she hit him in the chest. "But to be honest, I can't see how yours could get any better than it already is Bae." He said caressing her breast and squeezing her nipples between his fingers.

"Mhm you sure know how to --- oooh...change the subject huh?" she moaned.

"Lainy," he said getting her attention.

"Yes?"

"Screw me Bae." He said before closing his luscious lips around her nipple sucking hard.

Her pussy jumped, instantly getting soaked as she did just what her man said...after wrapping him up of course.

Chapter 9

Getting What's Yours

Tre pulled up to the address the GPS directed him to and looked around. He wasn't from the hood but he knew his way around one and this definitely was the hood…the rough part at that. There were dealers on the corners, crack fiends wandering up and down the street looking for a way to get their next fix, teenage girls wearing next to nothing. Most of them were already pushing baby strollers, carrying kids on their hips or in their bellies and by the looks of things even more would be doing the same by this time next year. Tre shook his head as he got out of the car, he now knew why Zi never allowed her girls to visit her…she didn't want them seeing how she lived. Before he could get to the sidewalk three dope boys had already run up on him trying to get a sell.

"Aye yo, do I look like I smoke that shit bruh?" he asked them.

"Looks can be deceiving my nig, you do have some functional crackheads y'know." One of the young dudes said.

"Sheit, you ain't saying nothing with that shit there dude, I got an uncle who drive a BMW, owns his own house and a couple of businesses and that nigga smoke more rock than a lil' bit so what's up? You need a hit or wha'?" he asked Tre again.

"Naw, I'm good. I don't get down like that, and for real…y'all need to be more careful who y'all running up on like that, I could've been po' po' or something." He schooled them.

"You must not know nothing but where you at my nig…them pigs know betta than to come 'round here. We'll roast they ass for sure dude."

"Word," his little homie cosigned dapping him up.

"Yo, if you ain't coppin' what the fuck you doing 'round here anyway? You lost or something, 'cause if so this the wrong place to be lost at I can tell you that now…especially driving that nice car you rolling in." said the smallest one of the crew.

"I'm actually here to see a friend of mine, this is the address I have for her so here I am…that's a'ight with you lil' man?" Tre said laughing.

"Only people live here is them dykes Zi and Lolo, them two don't fuck with no niggas so I know you ain't fuckin' one of them." Said the taller one of the three. "I don't know who them flowers for in ya car but if you think that's gonna work you trippin'. You know how much money niggas be offering to trick off on them two? Flowers ain't 'bouta getcha nowhere playboy." They laughed.

"Well I don't know who Lolo is, but I do know Zi and have for a very long time, as far as the flowers go…I guess we'll just have to see huh. Watch me get my pimpin' on." He smirked getting the flowers out of the car and walking toward the house where Zi lived. Tre opened the gate, made his way to the door and rang the bell. He'd seen Zi's car in the rundown carport so he knew she was there.

****

"Now who the hell is that?" Zi said aloud, walking to the door, her niece and roommate Lo was at work at the community center she helped run for underprivileged children in between her poetry and singing gigs and no one usually came over without calling first. As she stood on tiptoe to peep out the peephole she couldn't believe what she was seeing as she put her feet flat on the floor and shook her head to clear her vision. She looked again and started shaking. Tre Actlin was on the other side of her door! What…how…what the hell? Couldn't be, Tre was in the middle of the ocean on vacation with his family, there was no way he was standing on her porch right now…no damn way.

"Who?" Zi asked because her eyes had to be playing tricks on her.

"Zi open the door, you've already peeped two times so you know who it is."

"Tre?"

"You know anybody else who look this good?" he joked.

"Yep, definitely you." Zi muttered as she unlocked the door. "Tre what in the hell are you doing here?" she asked as she swung the door open.

"I told you that you'd be seeing me a lot sooner than you thought didn't I? As for what I'm doing here, I came to get you." He retorted.

"To get me? Are you crazy…you know what, I don't even know why I asked that when I already know the answer. Look, I'm not going with you Tre, I already told you that. Why your head so damn hard?"

"Said the kettle to the pot."

"Ughhh, you get on my last nerve Tre! What do you think is going to happen now, huh? You think I can just pick up and leave when I want to? Well news flash, I CAN'T…you wanna know why? Because I have a job and school and responsibilities and…"

"Okay STOP…I can't knock but so many excuses down at one time so let me get at the first 3 now. From what I recall you're on vacation right now, from school and work, as far as responsibilities go, technology is a beautiful thing, you can handle whatever needs to be done on the internet and if it's something concerning the house, I'm sure your roommate can handle it 'til you get back. Speaking of roommates…why your neighbors think y'all gay? You got something you wanna tell me?"

"What!? Gay? Where the hell you get that from? You ain't been here a good 10 minutes yet and motherfuckers already in your ear? Boy I swear people need to learn to mind their own business damn!" Zi spewed. "Who told you that shit," she asked headed for the door. "I'm 'bout to curse somebody's ass out right now…"

"Zi, calm down."

"Tre…you gonna answer my question or do I have to curse everybody who's out there out?"

"No, I'm not gonna tell you," he said grabbing her as she headed toward the door again. "And no you're not gonna curse anyone out either." He told her.

"Says who…you? Tre if you know what's good for you, you'd back off right about now 'cause I am .38 special hot boo."

".38 special hot Zi…really?"

"Hey, it sounds a whole lot better than dead dog serious." She said with an attitude.

"A'ight you got jokes huh?"

"I ain't in no laughing ass mood right now Tre."

"Well just to be clear, I'ont know 'bout the .38, but uh, I do think your special and let's not leave out hot…and in case you haven't noticed, I did bring flowers up in this piece even though I was warned by your little groupies that it wouldn't do me any good 'cause you're a dyke since you won't give up none of that good good even though niggas tryna cake off on you and Lulu." Tre said, trying to keep a straight face.

"See, you just gonna keep running with this shit right? Okay so let's clear the air once and for all in case there is ANY doubt in your mind…I like, enjoy, appreciate, drool over, get moist by, take pleasure in and receive pleasure from men and more specifically from their penises…are we clear? And it's Lolo, not Lulu jackass and she's not a dyke either, she's my niece but these assholes 'round here so focused on tryna get in all the pussy they can get that they never bothered to get to know any more than the fact that we're two females living together who won't give none of their trifling, broke down asses the time of day. Ewww, get real." She said giving him the screw face.

"Don't frown ya face up at me baby girl, I ain't the one spreading rumors about you." Tre joked.

"Whatever Tre, you can believe what you want, it don't matter to me one way or the other."

"Damn Zi, a nigga can't joke around with you now? It's like that? It ain't even that serious, I know you and I also know you want me too bad to give anybody else a second look…I don't care how pretty she is!"

"Tre I swear on everything I love, if you don't…"

"I quit," Tre said in between laughs. "come here Zi."

"Hell no!"

"Quit playin' girl and come here."

"I said, hell no. What part of that don't you understand? If you want me then you come to me." She responded crossing her arms over her chest and leaning back on one leg.

"You should know by now that I don't have a problem doing that, shit I flew all the way here to do just that. Now it's your turn…if you want me, come here." He said wanting to know where she stood.

"Is this one of your 'dead dog serious' moments?" Zi questioned.

"It is."

Zi wrestled with herself for a moment, trying to figure out if she really wanted to cross that line with Tre, because she knew without a doubt that if she did there would be no turning back and that scared her to her core. Zi's last relationship had ended horribly, causing her to have to get a restraining order and eventually press charges against her ex. In the end she just packed up her things and moved to a different state, because even though he was locked up, he still had people watching her and reporting everything she did and every move she made. When he got reports he didn't like he'd send her threatening mail or call her through a third party spazzing out on her not caring that she was turning over all of the evidence to the police thereby adding more time to his sentence. Zi had changed her number three times and he still managed to get it every time. After asking Tre to get his best friend Smiley to do some research, she found out that one of his cousins worked at the cell phone company she used and she reported it to her carrier and then, to be on the safe side she changed carriers altogether. Since then it had just been her and her niece Kelona and she wasn't sure if she was ready to get that involved with anyone again. On the other hand, she'd been crushing on Tre since the first time she met him but down played it not wanting to start something with him when they lived in two different states. Tre was too fine and women were always trying to get with him and it wasn't like he was trying to push them away, there was no way she was gonna give him a chance to hurt her by cheating with another girl. But that was then, she'd matured over the years and so had Tre apparently…surprise, surprise. Maybe they could make it work, maybe not but the only way she would find out was to give him a chance, and looking at him in her front room, sitting on the arm of her couch looking finer than frog hair she made up her mind to follow her intuition and give him…no them a chance.

"Well?"

"Boy chill, I'm coming…damn." She replied cutting her eyes at him.

"Your enthusiasm is touching. It warms my heart to hear the warmth in your voice." Tre responded sarcastically.

"See me and you gonna have some serious problems 'cause I am not the one Tre."

"Yes you are."

"Excuse me?" she said finally walking over to him, eyebrows raised ready to go toe to toe.

"You are the one…for me." He answered folding her in his arms.

"You sure about that? 'Cause once you open this door, you're going through, even if I have to drag your ass."

"Sheeit, if anybody is gonna need to be dragged it's your stubborn ass. I'm already on the other side waiting for you…you coming or what?" Tre taunted Zi.

"Yeah a'ight, I hear you talking that big boy shit but let me tell you something right now Tre…if you hurt me, I'm gonna hurt you…physically. Like take a bat and crack every bone in your body, run you over with my car, shoot you in the kneecaps…"

"Okay, okay damn Zi…thought about this much?" he said looking at her questioningly.

"No, that was just off the top of my head, but the fact still remains…I meant everything I just said. If you ain't ready for this or you're not sure this is what you really want then don't…"

"Zi, stop working yourself up okay? I'm a grown ass man and I know what and WHO I want. All this babble you talking about ain't 'bout shit a'ight because you already know where I stand. You're the one who's been running from this, not me. After I ran into you in Orlando and saw what that nigga was putting you through, I gave you a shoulder to cry on and an ear to listen when you were to ashamed to talk to your girls about what was going on with you. I gave you time to get yourself together after you finally came to your senses and left that asshole you were fuckin' with alone. I even did as you asked and had Smiley look into your situation, because I wanted you to have peace of mind and to know that I was there for you whenever you needed me. Moreover, I did all of that without ever breaking your confidence, now do you really think I'd do all of that if I didn't want to be here, if I didn't want to be with you? Do I look like the kind of guy who would put in all of that work without earning his reward?"

"Yeah you put in work alright. Don't think I don't know you were the one who beat the crap outta Mar-Lo either."

"I'ont know what you talkin' 'bout." Tre said innocently.

"Oh you know exactly what I'm talkin' 'bout Tre, that innocent shit don't work with me. I done watched you use that look to get your way too many times so uhn uhn, don't even try it."

"No haps?"

"None."

"A'ight, yeah I whipped his ass, and I'd do it again. You got a problem with that?"

"None at all." Zi replied.

"Good, now that we've got that out of the way, how 'bout you go get your stuff together so we can ride out."

"No."

"No?"

"Yeah, you know…the opposite of yes."

"Funny Zi, why we still dancing in this circle when you already know I'ma get my way?"

"Tre, I can't just up and leave whenever I please. I do have responsibilities and I have to make sure Lolo is straight and…"
"Oh boy, please stop before you get on a roll. What responsibilities are you talking about? Maybe we can get them squared away before we leave."

"My niece for one."

"Problem solved. While you're packing get some stuff together for Lelo too."

"It's Lolo, Dodo and really? Are you sure that your parents aren't going to mind? I'on know about this Tre."

"You don't have to know, I do and who do you think helped me get here so quickly to pick you up? Stop procrastinating Zi, chop chop let's go."

80

"You're rushing me but we still have to wait on Lo to get home and as far as packing for her, fagetaboutit, that girl has a style of her own and nothing I put together would work for her so I'm not even about to waste my time."

"Give me your phone."

"I beg your pardon."

"You got something to hide?"

"No."
"Then give your phone. I'll call Lolo while you're packing."

"You think I'm slow or something? I know how to multitask."

"That's not the point."

"Then what is?"

"Look if you call her she's gonna think you're playing and y'all are gonna waste about an hour going back and forth over who's lying and who's telling the truth. But if I call her, off your phone she will immediately know it's real and I can answer any questions she may have about where we're going, the CAILIN or anything else pertaining to the trip. Now can I get your phone?"

"I guess," she replied, taking the lock off her phone before handing it to him.

"Before you go do you think you can put these flowers in some water before they die."

"Nope, I'm taking those with me."

"Why?"

"Because you bought them for me to enjoy and I can't enjoy them if they're in here and I'm not."

Tre cracked a smile and licked his lips while looking at Zi as she headed down the hallway.

"Need any help?" he asked as she turned into her room.

"I'm good Boo."

"No doubt, and believe me I can't wait to find out." Tre replied licking his lips.

Zi paused in her door before looking back at Tre, head tilted to the side she cracked a smile before responding.

"No doubt." She said while looking at the bulge outlined against his jeans. Zi winked her eye at Tre, walked in her room and promptly locked her door…she wasn't taking any chances, 'cause if Tre walked through her door the only thing that would be getting packed was her…with a whole lot of him.

Chapter 10

In Need of Some Sexual Healing

"Did you enjoy yourself tonight?" Ra asked Devah as they left the island's nightclub where they'd spent the last few hours dancing off the dizzying array of local appetizers they'd indulged in while watching the sun set over the ocean, laughing, talking and people watching. Ra had Devah laughing so hard with his funny quips and impersonations her stomach muscles were sore.

"I did indeed, especially after meeting up with the Marteness's." she said laughing and shaking her head.

At one point in their evening he'd gotten up to dance with an older lady after she'd worn her husband out on the dance floor. Twirling her around, two-stepping and doing the cha-cha with her, ending the dance with a dip that the older woman ate up like a fruit basket, wrapping her arms around his neck and laying a kiss right on his lips! Ra had Devah laughing out loud when he looked up at the husband, wiggled his eyebrows, twisted her wedding ring around and tucked her hand in the crook of his arm heading toward the exit…his wife even had the audacity to wave good-bye. After everyone got a good laugh at them, the husband shook hands and thanked Ra for taking over and saving him from passing out on the dance floor and embarrassing himself. Devah looked on from their table at the three of them approaching as he brought them over to the table and introduced the couple to her.

"Bae, this is Blanchay and Tavis Marteness, and this is my lady Dawnesha Actlin."

"Hello, how do you do?" Devah addressed the lovely couple.

"Fine dear and thank you for allow your handsome young man to make an old woman's evening." Blanchay said smiling.

"Not to mention an old man's night, now she'll be too tired to drag me back on the dance floor." Tavis joked.

"No problem at all, thank you for letting him burn off some energy since I can't."

"Why not? Are your feet hurting you?" Blanchay asked glancing at Devah's stilettos. "By the way those are fierce honey."

"Thank you, and no it's not because of that it's because every time I stand up…so does he." Devah laughed.

"Hunh?"

"Never mind, I'm just teasing Ra."

"Yeah, but we gon' see who gets the last laugh." Ra replied behind half closed eyes.

"Ohh, I get it now. That dress is a complete turn on and fits your body beautifully…if I could still get away with wearing things like that I definitely would."

"What are you talking about Mrs. Marteness…"

"Please, call me Chay."

"Ok Ms. Chay, you have a lovely shape and are most definitely wearing that outfit." Devah complimented her.

"Thank you dear, but the sisters are tired and what used to bounce barely jiggles anymore." Chay said theatrically.

"No disrespect, but that's far from tired and stiff," Ra said eyeing her, "you are what they were referring to when they used the term 'brick house' back in the day."

"Oh, trust me she was and still is, don't pay her no nevermind. That's just her way of fishing for compliments; she's still got a freak'um dress or two in the closet." Tavis said 'causing them to laugh.

"What you know about a freak'um dress Mr...."

"Just call me Tavis, and I know because I married a freak."

Devah's mouth fell open and she turned to look at Ra who was high fiving Tavis.

"Really Ra?"

"What bae, I was just giving the man his props." He said innocently.

"It's ok, it's not like he's lying or anything." Chay said waving the men's actions off, "Listen, back in our day my husband was the man on campus you hear me. Every girl and some teachers mind you, wanted to be the lucky one who got to be with him and trust me he took full advantage of it too. But when it was all said and done and he set his sights on me well I had to be the opposite of everything he was used to. Once he realized I wasn't gonna be an easy catch he started paying more attention to me versus my body. And when the time was right…on our wedding night of course, he got the gift no other man has ever touched. Luckily he was a knowledgeable teacher and I was an apt student because I took everything he taught me and flipped it on him! He's been trying to keep up ever since." She laughed. Tavis shook his head at his wife's antics and then shrugged his shoulders.

"Next time I'll know to keep some secrets to myself." He said.

"You won't be able to hang with her either." His wife replied.

"Do you have someone in mind already?" Devah asked jokingly.

"No one in particular dear, just his imaginary trophy wife that's all."

"I see."

"Yes, you see Tavis is under the mistaken impression that after having been with one woman for the last 35…"

"36 Sweetness."

"I meant 36 years, that he's entitled to a trophy wife when he turns 60 which is in 3 more years. I allow him to have his little fantasy but little does he know, I've got a few fantasies of my own I wouldn't mind living out and as Ra stated earlier ain't nothing wrong with this body here baby … I'm still a brick house!" she said, side eyeing her husband who had the nerve to look surprised.

"This is the first I'm hearing of any of this. A few huh?" he said looking at his wife contemplatively. "I think we have a few things to talk about, if you two will excuse us, the missus and I have some things we need to work out in private."

"By all means." Ra said with a knowing smirk

"Well it was nice meeting you both, you guys make a great couple, you remind me of my parents." Devah said, "And you Mr. Tavis, you already have your trophy wife."

"Don't I know it." He responded wrapping his arm around his wife's waist and giving her a quick kiss.

"You better." His wife replied tapping him on his ass.

"Let your freak flag fly!" Ra said raising his glass in the air. "It's 'bout to be on tonight." He teased them.

"Like Donkey Kong." Said Tavis.

Devah and Chay fell out laughing at their men. As they exchanged hugs and numbers Chay whispered to Devah that her husband had played right into her hands responding exactly how she'd wanted him to and she gave her a wink and said "Reverse psychology…works every time!" and the Marteness's were on their way.

"Yeah, they were hilarious."

"I also enjoyed the walk on the beach, the serenade," she cut her eyes, referring to when he paid a street musician to play the tune to 'Freak Me' by Silk and he sang it to her in front of a shit load of strangers embarrassing her to no end. "and finally being able to hit the dance floor without you mean muggin' every man in the building. That shit don't make any kind of sense Ra, what's up with all of that. You are far from being insecure so talk to me." Devah said as they headed back to the yacht.

"Ain't nothing up, I just didn't want all them niggas eyeing you like…"

"YOU?" Devah finished for him.

"Yeah, exactly…like me. And I *know* what I'm thinking when I'm looking at you, I don't even want to imagine what they're thinking."

"Who cares?"

"I do."

"Why?"

"Because…I just do."

"That's not an answer."

"It is to me."

Devah thought about what Chay had whispered in her ear.

"So let me ask you this, if I were to do the same thing to you every time a woman looked your way that shit would get old real quick wouldn't it?" she asked him.

Ra thought about it for a few and realized that she was right, that would get old quick and piss him off to be honest.

"Yeah, you're right. I wouldn't like it one bit and I apologize for doing it to you. I was being a possessive asshole and it's not a good look."

"No it's not."

"Forgive me?" he asked pulling her close and sucking softly on her neck.

"I'll think about it."

"Oh yeah?"

"Mmh hhm." She moaned as he kissed her on her lips.

"What can I do to make it up to you?" he asked looking at her through lust filled eyes.

"Make my freak flag fly." She whispered in his ear, running a finger down his erection and squeezing the head.

Ra leaned back to look her in her eyes and make sure she wasn't playing no games, he had every intention on seducing her tonight, he just didn't think she'd be the one initiating the process.

"Are you sure bae?" he asked licking his lips.

Devah turned around and headed for the yacht, her every step all the answer he needed as he rushed to catch up with her, grabbed her hand and practically had her running to keep up with each step he took.

"Ra, can you please slow down before I fall? These shoes cost a fortune and if I break a heel…"

"I'll buy you a new pair." He said stabbing the elevator button repeatedly, impatient for the doors to open. When he headed for the stairs Devah dug her heels in.

"Uhn uhn, I am not taking the stairs. Stop being so impatient, I ain't going nowhere." She said as the elevator doors slid open. Ra held the doors and waited for Devah to enter before stepping in the enclosure and pressing her floor. He leaned against the wall and reached for her, pulling her between his opened legs and settling her on him intimately.

"Are you sure you're ready for this? And I need a real answer because some real shit is about to go down when we get to your room, so if you don't think you can handle this," he said grinding into her, "you need to let me know now."

"I've got a few things to learn I'm sure but I'm an apt student, I pick up real quick, especially if it's a favorite subject. So to answer your question, I'm as ready as I'm gonna get. I want you, I have since the day you walked in the kitchen at Stance and Shane's and I don't want to wait anymore. I'm tired of fighting my feelings and my attraction to you, of waking up out of my sleep wet for you and masturbating to thoughts of you…I want you to make love to me Ra." Devah said, making Ra harder and harder with every word out of her delectable mouth.

"Damn you be waking up wet for me Ma? That shit's a turn on for real… at least I know I ain't the only one having wet dreams. On the real bae, you had me feeling like a little boy nutting on myself at night." He said as the elevator doors slid open and they stepped out heading to her room. The two stopped short as they saw her uncle Zell sitting outside her room sleeping against the wall. Devah started giggling and Ra shook his head as he took her key card and quietly unlocked the door. After they were both in the room, he slammed the door hard enough to give Zell a headache, a heart attack or both and then locked the door.

"Hey!" Zell yelled from the other side of the door as he listened to them laughing at him. "You just remember what I told you young blood." He warned Ra, grabbing his chair and cursing himself for falling asleep.

Devah fell out laughing even more, the laughter breaking some of the sexual tension between them.

"Exactly what did he tell you?" she asked between giggles.

"Not to do anything he would do."

"Well hell, that doesn't leave much, does it?"

"That's exactly what I said."

'Uh huh, what else did you tell him?" she said, no longer laughing as she stepped out of her heels and backed up toward the bedroom, turning on some music and selecting her love jams playlist.

"That I wouldn't do any more than you let me." He responded.

"Well then, that opens the door to all kinds of possibilities then." She replied, unzipping her dress.

"Yes, it does. Stop," he said from the doorway, as Devah looked at him questioningly. "I've been wanting to get you out of that dress all night. Please…allow me." He said walking over to her and sliding the zipper the rest of the way down, then untying the top so that the dress fell down in a puddle at her feet. As Ra stepped back to admire the splendor that was standing before him he felt himself lengthening in size to an extent he'd never experienced before. He'd never wanted any woman as much as he craved Devah and he was suddenly afraid of the thought that he could lose control of himself and hurt Devah with his desire for her. At 5'6 and kissed by the sun all over, she was a bronzed beauty with full luscious breasts and an ass he could get lost in. Devah was every man's fantasy with every dip and curve in perfect proportion to her body.

"Ra?" Devah said, as she watched the myriad of emotions run across his face. "Are you ok?" she asked breaking him out of his trance. Ra licked his lips and walked back to her as he unbuttoned his shirt.

"I'm good Ma." He said as she moved his hands to finish the task.

"You sure, 'cause you looked a little scared over there. Don't worry baby, I won't hurt you." She teased.

"Shit I ain't worried about that, I'm more concerned about hurting you. I ain't never in my life been this turned on, this brick for a female in my life…EVER. Bae you just don't know what you do to me." He told her as he nibbled on her lips.

"I guess I'll find out tonight then huh?" she asked before inserting her tongue into his mouth and pushing his shirt to the floor. Devah pulled his t-shirt over his head and then continued the kiss as her hands wandered all over his lightly haired chest, moving lower and lower until he stopped her. Ra put Devah's arms around his neck and lifted her up so she could wrap her legs around his waist. He walked to her bed and laid her down on the edge before breaking the kiss and heading for her breasts. As he put one nipple in his mouth they both moaned in appreciation as he laved the chocolate colored tit with his tongue before sucking her nipple, causing tremors to radiate from her chest down to her core. Devah's stomach muscles started tensing as he moved from one breast to the other, stimulating her with his fingers each time he switched. When Ra squeezed both her breasts together and lightly bit them at the same time, Devah did something she'd never done before; she had an orgasm from breast stimulation…an intense one at that. The shudders raked up and down her body as Ra made his way to her Hello Kitty and with one long swipe of his tongue had her jumping off the bed to get away from the sensations running rampantly through her. Ra grabbed her thighs and lifted them up as he pulled her back to the edge of the bed and locked his arms around her holding her open in front of him.

"Where you trying to go Ma? I thought you wanted this."

"Ra, I can't take it, my body is on overload. Every time you touch me it feels like volts of electricity are running through my body. That shit is nerve racking, what are you doing to me?" Devah panted as he locked on to her clit and massaged it with his lips and tongue switching it up to give her long laps of his tongue over her sensitive core until she erupted again and again. Just when she thought she would pass out from the nonstop stimulation he released her and stood up to remove the rest of his clothes. Devah immediately balled up into a fetal position, trembling in the middle of the bed.

"You already trembling and you ain't get the realness yet." Ra said coming up out of the rest of his clothing. "This right here," he said holding almost 9 inches of dick almost as thick as his wrist in his hand. "Bae, this is as real as it gets. You want this, you gotta come and get it." He said removing his hand and letting his dick curve to the left against his hipbone. Devah stared at the massive organ, wondering if she should change her mind now that she could actually see what was about to tear her insides apart. She thought Tres was huge and even compared to Ra he was still working with something, but honestly, there was no comparison because Ra won on size hands down. What the hell am I doing comparing dick sizes at a time like this, Devah thought to herself, besides from what I've heard it's not the size that counts; it's what you do with it that matters. And Devah was curious enough to want to know if Ra was as good as he said he was despite her fear of his size. She unfurled from the center of the bed and with much trepidation walked over to him.

"Now what?" she asked quivering before him.

"Now you get what you came for. Touch me; let me feel your hands on me." Ra replied gutturally.

Devah reached out with shaky hands to touch him, his dick felt hard as steel yet satiny smooth. She grabbed hold of him with both hands, she used the cum from the tip of his dick to lubricate her hands as she slid them up and down his length. Ra threw his head back and let out a deep groan of pleasure as Devah got into it, squeezing her hands and rubbing her thumb over his head so more cum would leak out. When he felt her grab his balls with one hand and blow on his dick with her mouth he almost lost it. His legs were unsteady as she turned him toward the bed and pushed him down. Before he could lift his head up to see what she was doing, she was on her knees between his legs engulfing the head of his penis in her mouth. The growl that came from the back of Ra's throat was so primal it sounded like a wounded animal. The noises he made just did something to Devah and she wanted to keep him singing his tunes to her in harmony with Tank's song 'Fucking Wit' Me' so she licked him from the base of his penis to the tip where she swallowed his cream that came leaking from within. When she finally placed him back in her mouth, Ra slowly pushed to the back of her throat and held her head as he began to pump in her open mouth. As he tried to go further, she gagged, she didn't know how to deep throat since she'd only learned the basics having stopped giving Tres head after he continued to cheat on her, she figured he could get it from one of his sidelines.

"Breathe bae and open up your mouth some more." Ra coached her. "Yeah now loosen your throat muscles and swallow…ssss, shit yeah. Uhn uhn, don't do that, hold ya head back some so I can slide down a little more. Damn bae, that shit feel good." He said as he started stroking his dick in and out, little by little. Devah swallowed again and Ra went a little further than he meant to, causing her to gag and he pulled out so she could breathe. When Devah leaned over to finish her lesson Ra pulled her up.

"Naw bae, you 'bout to unman me as it is. Damn, I knew that mouth was good for more than just talking shit." Ra teased her.

"Oh shut up before I change my mind."

"That's on you Ma, you the one gon be missing out on all this goodness." He said wrapping his hand around his pole of delight and stroking it.

"Ooh, damn that's sexy right there." Devah said watching him stroke himself as he pulled more juice out of the tip.

"Just the head." Devah said as she leaned over and sunk her lips around him, sucking his essence down her throat.

"Naw bae, I can't hold it back this time, and I don't want the first time I let loose in you to be in your mouth, I want ya other set of lips wrapped around my dick." He said easing her off of him and reaching for the XL condoms he placed on the night stand when he was getting undressed.

"You bought the largest box they had in'it?" Devah joked.

"Actually I bought two." Was his reply

"You must plan on being real busy when I go back to Charlotte." She stated.

"I plan on being real busy with you…in Charlotte or Charleston. It don't matter to me, you the only one getting this dick so stop stalling so I can play hide and seek with that pussy."

Devah giggled at that image not realizing that Ra was arranging her on the bed so that he could enter her until he'd placed the head at the entrance of her vagina and started pushing.

"Shit just got real huh?" Ra joked.

"Oooouch!" she responded

"It ain't even in yet Devah."

"And yet it still hurts RaShiem."

96

"RaShiem huh," he smirked, "you want me to stop?"

"What you think?"

"I think if that hurt, then this," he said grabbing her shoulders, palms up to hold her in place, "is really gonna hurt." He grunted as he pushed even more inside her stretching her wide open and bringing tears to her eyes and a slight scream from her lips. Ra bent down to swallow her cries with his mouth, kissing her until she responded back. He lifted his head up to lick the tears from the sides of her face.

"You a'ight?" he asked looking in her eyes.

"I feel like I've been ripped in half and set on fire."

"All that bae, you don't think you're exaggerating just a little bit?"

"Hell naw, let me shove 8 inches of thick dick up you and see how you like it."

Ra laughed at Devah's tantrum.

"Closer to 9 inches bae."

"Ra I don't care if it was 4 inches you wouldn't be able to take it either!" Devah exclaimed.

"My body ain't made for this type of shit, but yours is, so relax and enjoy it bae. I promise you I'mma make you feel real, real good. Just let me do what I do." He said as he feed her some more of his dick. "Damn bae your shit tight as fuck, you sure you ain't no virgin?" he quipped causing her to laugh and loosen up some more. Ra took advantage of the distraction and sunk his dick all the way in making her body tense up as she tried to stiff arm him.

"Ra that's too much, it feels like you're gonna break something bae I can't move."

"You remember what I told you that day this all started?"

"You said a lot that day." She remembered.

"I told you I was going to blaze new paths, reach places that nigga ain't never touched before. I meant that shit, bae." He said while long stroking her pussy at an easy pace and making sure to apply pressure to her swollen clit every time he pushed the bulbous tip of his dick back in her tight cooch.

"Ooh shit bae that feels so good…so, so good." Devah moaned as the pain subsided and pleasure took over her whole body.

"I told you I wasn't no joke, but you ain't wanna believe me so I had to show you." Ra said while grinding in her deep, all the while looking in her eyes as their bodies moved in sensuous dips and swirls over the silken sheets.

"Mmm, you're sooo deep in my pussy I can feel your dick tapping my spine." Devah moaned in pleasure. Ra laughed as he eased up on her womb, easing out and just giving her the tip to rotate on. Devah took a deep breath and let it out slowly.

"What's wrong bae?" Ra asked her.

"Nothing," she said in a vulnerable voice closing her eyes.

"Devah…"

"Yes?"

"Look at me."

She looked up at his face and said again, "Yes?"

"DEVAH," he said with a little extra bass in his voice as he stopped in mid stroke staring at her.

"WHAT? Damn, how many times do you want me to answer you?"

"I want you to look at me," he said stressing the word look.

"I am…"

"No you're not, I can't see you clearly if you're not looking me in my eyes, I feel like you're closing yourself off to me and I can't see what you're thinking or feeling when you do that and you can't see what I'm saying to you by looking in my mouth… you need to look in my eyes if you want to hear what I'm saying because that's where my truth resides, understand?

"Yes."

"Good because I'm only gonna say this one more time…Devah."

"Yes?" She said while looking in his eyes.

"I don't want you to hold back when you talk to me, I want you to be yourself at all times…" he paused for a second and then said, "well maybe not allllll the time." she gasped out loud and then she hit him.

"Ouch! I was just playing bae."

"Yeah well you betta watch what you're saying, I ain't scared of you." She warned.

"I don't want you to be scared of me; I can make you tremble without fear…just like you're doing right now." He said while flexing his penis in her tight, hot and silky wet pussy, groaning when she gripped him tightly and massaged his length and thickness until she shuddered, on the verge of cumming.

"Mmh mmm mmm, damn that shit feels good, you got the silkiest pussy I've ever been in."

"Don't remind me I'm just another notch on your belt." Ra looked at her for a few seconds then he shook his head.

"Naw Divalicious, you're not a notch at all…you're the whole damn belt, ain't no room for anybody else to squeeze in here... you feel me?"

She nodded her head.

"Good, so like I was saying earlier," he said stroking her deeply, "I don't want there to be any secrets or miscommunication between us. If you want to know something ask, but I'mma keep it a hunnid with you EVERY time so look me in my eyes and ask me anything you want, but don't ask if you really don't want to know the answer. Now I see you a little nervous, acting all shy and shit but you gon have to get over that real quick." he said while grinding on her spot, "I'm bouta bring your freak out the closet," he said while increasing his pace, "'cause I know there's a kinky ass…"

"Oh shit!" Devah said in between moaning his name,

"...freak deep inside you,"

"RA! Unhhh, unhhh...oh shit ba-ba-ba," she couldn't get the word baby out to save her soul. His dick felt so good she was incoherent and out of her mind with pleasure.

"...and I plan on getting to know her," Ra continued while placing her feet on his chest and twining his fingers with hers and holding her arms above her head, straight beasting in her sweetness driving her crazy. "...before the night is over. So you might as well let Ms. Divalicious come out and play 'cause Mr. Raw is definitely ready to meet her," he said before putting her legs to the side and sliding in and out of her while talking dirty. Devah's moans of pleasure filled the sex scented room driving Ra wild. He placed her flat on her back and when she spread her legs to place one on the other side of his body, opening herself up to him, well, he took advantage of the opportunity presented to him as he started thrusting in and out of her with short, deep thrusts, lifting up every time he hit bottom to make sure he tapped that spot for her. Ra told her to get on her knees making sure to keep pressure on her swollen, sensitive clit as he arched her back, gripped her hips and plunged in and out of her hot heat. When Devah tried to run from the dick, putting her arm back and stiff arming him with no success, he just stroked harder and deeper until she got the message and moved her arm. Finally she was able to slide down on her stomach and try to roll away from him but he followed and they both groaned out loud from the different sensations they were feeling from this particular position. She was already tight as fuck around his dick but this position made her cooch so tight it was like fucking a virgin, he could barely move so he braced his knees on the mattress and locked his toes on the edge of the bed and fucked her so hard and so good she was crying and begging him not to stop at the same damn time and he had no intention of doing so until they both burst from the explosion that had been building in them for so long…until then he would continue to feed the flame. With each thrust, grind, kiss, suck, look and word he had her losing grip on reality. And surprisingly, she was good with that.

Chapter 11

Lies of Omission

Lainy looked out at the ocean as she contemplated her future. She'd never planned on telling Shell about her…their twins Lain and Shellona, because she'd been close to letting her aunt and uncle adopt them. They'd been helping her raise the children in Myrtle Beach SC since she'd given birth to them. When she'd left them to move back to Charleston to start her business, it had been on a trial basis. But the last six months had been extremely hard on her being away from the twins for days, sometimes weeks at a time, each visit getting harder and harder to walk away from. She knew she was going to have to make up her mind real soon, actually she knew she didn't have much of a decision to make, she was going to have to tell Shell about them when they got back home. She knew that this could potentially blow up in her face, her keeping such a huge and significant secret from him, but she was counting on the bond they'd created with one another to get them through. Lainy felt the hairs on the back of her neck stand up and she glanced around to see who or what had caused the sensation. One of the crewmen was behind her clearing off tables; he averted her eyes when she looked at him as if he didn't want her to see him. She could sense the hostility coming from him and something about his body language seemed familiar to Lainy but she couldn't place it. She knew that wherever she knew him from, it wasn't from the yacht because the staff ran so efficiently you rarely saw them.

"Good afternoon." She spoke trying to get him to face her so she could get a good look at him. He waved his hand and kept putting dishes in his little gray plastic tub never once turning around.

"How long have you worked on the CAILIN?" Lainy asked, but before he could respond Shell came through the door looking for her.

"Well hello."

"Hello." She responded.

"I thought you would be too tired to get out of the bed after last night."

"Hell you did all the work all I had to do was enjoy myself, which I did…immensely." Lainy said softly, not wanting the crewman to hear their personal conversation. Shane on the other hand…

"Well you know, I made a promise to make that first one up to you for the rest of the night and I'm a man of my word. But don't worry, tonight it's your turn to do all the work." He said smiling.

"Well if that's the case the night will be ending very early. You already know I have no experience except with you."

"Oh don't worry; I will be instructing your every move until you pass all tests with straight A's. My dick's getting hard just thinking about it, let's go downstairs and practice." Shell said grinding into Lainy.

"Shell stop, he can see you and I know he can hear you. The more I whisper the louder you get. I don't want that man all in our business."

"Who?" Shane asked looking around. "Oh, he ain't paying us no attention so why you worried about him? Fuck him."

"Oh you just on a roll today huh? Give you a little bit of cooch and you wanna fuck everybody." Lainy said laughing at Shell's expression.

"Naw bae, this here," he said placing her hand over his erection, "is all for you. And you know you gonna get it for that remark right? You laughing now but I'm gonna make you regret indicating some ratchet ass shit like that…watch me."

"Now Shell, you know I was just playing."

"Of course, but you can't play like that with me without suffering some consequences so just be prepared."

"For what?" Lainy asked nervously.

"You'll soon find out." He smirked.

"Will this involve any pain."

"Only as much as you can take."

Lainy thought back to last night and this morning and all of the painfully delicious things he'd done to her and smiled.

"Well in that case I'd rather have my punishment now instead of later."

"I know, and that's why I'mma make your ass wait 'til *I'm* ready…not you." He replied grinding into her and brushing his thumbs back and forth over her nipples.

"Shell stop playing, you standing here getting me all worked up and then you don't want to deliver, that ain't right."

Shell gripped Lainy's left breast in his hand leaned his head down and sucked hard on her nipple, right through her bikini top causing her knees to buckle from the pull to her core. He held her up with his body as she leaned against the railing shaking, trying to stay upright.

"Shell…" she moaned.

"Yes?" he answered her.

"Let's go back to your room."

"Nope."

Lainy's eyes popped open.

"No?"

"You heard me."

"Pleassse Shell." She begged grabbing the front of his pants and caressing him.

They both turned around when they heard shattering glass to see the crewman squinting down to pick up the broken pieces with his fingers.

"Yo, my man…you a'ight?" Shell asked, heading toward him to check. "You look like you're bleeding, don't touch that, I'll have someone come pick that up. You go to the infirmary so they can fix that up for you." He said as he pushed a button on the device attached to his belt. "I need someone on the main deck to clean up some broken glass. Bring gloves and a hazard bag, there's been some minor bloodshed." He stated before pausing to listen to his earpiece, "Yeah it was the new guy," he answered before adding, "he's headed to the infirmary now. Is there something I need to know about?" he listened again, "A'ight, I expect a full report when you do." He said ending the conversation. Looking thoughtfully at the exit the crewman had disappeared through.

"Shell…is everything alright?" Lainy asked puzzled by his one-sided conversation.

"Huh, oh it's nothing for you to worry about…everything's good."

"Doesn't sound like it's all good, besides something about that guy bothers me. He gives me the creeps, don't ask why…he just does." Throwing up her hand and forestalling the inevitable question he was waiting to ask.

"Did he say something to you?"

"No."

"Then what about him bothered you?"

"I guess him…his presence. It's like I could feel some kind of animosity coming from him and something about him just seemed familiar, but I can't place it…"

"Why didn't you say something when I first came out here?"

"Because you distracted me." She replied, as Shell reached out to distract her some more, one of the crewman came on deck to clean up the mess.

"Excuse, me folks I'll be outta ya way in a few minutes. How you two love birds doing this here fine morning?" Floyzelle Wiggins, head crewman, asked the two.

"We're doing good, how 'bout yourself…you keeping up with your medications?" Shell asked.

"Yes sir, and I appreciate you going out of your way to make sure of it too Shell, you alright with me sonny boy."

"No problem at all, gotta make sure you straight or nothing will get done around here." Shell teased him, "I made sure the pharmacy stocked up on plenty of pain medication to a'ight? You let me know if there's anything else I can do for you ok?"

"Oh, you've done more than enough. You two enjoy the rest of your day, I'm gonna dispose of this mess and check on Quin…something's off with that one, I just can't put my finger on it." He said shaking his head as he headed toward the exit.

I see I'm not the only one who thinks there's something wrong with him Lainy thought to herself. Something was really bothering her about the guy, her intuition was on high alert but she didn't know which way the danger would come…only that it would.

Shell knew something wasn't right, three people in the span of less than thirty minutes had said something was off with this Quin dude and he trusted and respected all three of them. He didn't know what it was about him that had them on edge but he was going to make it his business to find out real soon what was up with him because now that he thought about it, there was something familiar about ol' boy. He was gonna have a talk with Smiley as soon as he finished distracting Lainy some more.

Chapter 12

Blood is Thicker Than Water

   Smiley disconnected his earpiece after having talked to Shell and made his way to the infirmary, pretending to have hurt himself in the kitchen as an excuse to see the doctor. Once he found out who had been cut he knew this was his chance to find out everything he needed to know without alerting his target. The only people who knew who he was were the two families and Doc. He didn't want Doc to ask why he needed a sample of Quin's blood so he figured he'd get one of the bloody gauze used to stop the bleeding and run some test on it with the equipment he had set up in a private room in one of the master suites that was off limits to the rest of the crew. By tomorrow morning he'd know all there was to know about Mr. Quince Perkins. Smiley didn't know what it was about Quin that bothered him, only that something did and being who he was he was going to get to the bottom of it.

****

   Quin couldn't believe Lainy was acting like that, letting Shell touch her and begging him for sex! She was allowing him to do things she never even considered doing to him…how dare she play with his emotions like that…bitch! Fucking scandalous bitch, he'd show her who she was playing with he thought laughing to himself as he thought about how he'd do just that, he'd show them both what the fuck he was capable of Quin thought as all traces of laughter left him replaced with rage and hatred. Hell had no fury like a nigga who felt like he ain't had shit to lose because in the land of Quin one thing was for certain and two for sure…if he couldn't have Lainy NOBODY could, especially not that bitch ass Shellon Actlin. I'm about to wreak pure havoc in their lives, he thought to himself as he went about planning his revenge on the two people he felt were ruining his life. Shell took Lainy away from him and he was going to return the favor real soon and if anyone else got caught up in the madness…so be it, he had 99 problems giving a fuck wasn't one.

Chapter 13

Good Cop Gone For Good

      Brishay Frasier was enjoying some much needed time off from her job as lead detective in the North Charleston Police Department when she got a call from her ex-partner and friend Tijee "Smiley" Rollins. Smiley had left the department over 2 years ago because he'd been tired of the dirty cops making everyone else look bad, and after witnessing several cops beat the system time and time again he knew it was only a matter of time before he lost it and did something that would land him behind bars for defending yet another innocent citizens from his crooked brethren. That time came when he was called to a scene where a young 16 year old boy lay fighting for life after being beaten severely by several officers, one in particular an officer B. Oone was overly aggressive in the beating of the young man, claiming to have seen a gun that was never found and that the teenager was a part of a gang when in fact he was a part of a local rap group, made straight A's in school and played sports for his high school team. The young man had never been in trouble before and every officer involved went out of their way to make the young man out to be a gangbanger and when they were proven wrong not one offered an apology and each were given a slap on the wrist before being set back out on the streets to do it all over again. The day that happened and they came back to the precinct laughing, joking and high fiving to another job well done Smiley lost it and went berserk on Officer Oone who had the most to say and was the most invidious of the four. His mendacious lies and testimony is what helped to get the others off and Smiley had had enough of his bullshit so he gave him a dose of his own medicine and whipped his ass like he'd stole something from him and in truth he had, he'd stolen his sense of justice and faith in the North Charleston PD which in turn made him feel like he was fighting a losing battle and contributing to the delinquency of the department. After all was said and done, Smiley walked out of the doors of the NCPD with his dignity and morals intact, leaving behind the only things that mattered to him…his badge, his mentor Capt. L. T. Jones and his partner Shay. When Oone started hollering about pressing charges Capt. Larry T. Jones stepped in and with all the dirt and grime he had on Oone and the added threat of leaking all of his misdeeds to the press despite what Mayor Chumney had to say, Oone wisely declined to press charges. Smiley went on to open his own private investigation office and two years into it he not only had offices in Charleston and Columbia SC, he was opening up his third office in Raleigh NC. Brishay knew he was traveling with his best friend Tre and his family undercover and that if he was calling it might be important but hell she worked hard for the NCPD and just as hard for him part-time and she wanted to enjoy her vacation. Debating on whether or not to answer, her decision was made when her front door opened and her current plaything walked in. Making up her mind to call Smiley later on, she placed her phone on the side table and walked over to meet her hunk of delight halfway. As she wrapped her arms around his neck and he latched on to her pretty brown round she forgot all about Smiley.

****

Damn, Smiley swore as the phone went to voicemail, he hated leaving messages on shit that was this important as well as time sensitive but he knew he had no choice, Shay was the only one he trusted with this information and he knew how absolutely thorough she was when it came down to getting the bad guys. After leaving her a detailed message he hung up and called Shell.

"Yeah, what's up? You get what you need yet?" Shell answered, not wasting any time.

"I got a blood sample, now I'm just waiting on Shay to get back with me with the DNA results."

"What's the wait on that info?"

"I'm hoping sooner rather than later."

"You're hoping? Naw bruh you gotta do better than that. Tell me you gave Shay some sort of deadline. I mean you, Flossy and Lay have all said that you get a weird vibe from him which only validates what I've been feeling all along so I need you to tell me more than that." Shell said, his exasperation reflected in his tone of voice.

"Look bruh, I understand your frustration but in all honesty he hasn't done anything that we know of so this could very well turn out to be nothing. The fact that we all feel some type of way about him could just speak to his personality…he's not a very likable or sociable person which makes it hard to get a read on him but…"

"Smiley," Shell cut him off, "have you EVER gotten a bad vibe from a person and it turned out to be nothing?" he asked.

"Well it wasn't always what I thought it to be but it was always something." He clarified.

"As long as I've known you that sixth sense of yours has always been on point. When there are people who don't have that spidey sense still sensing something wrong I really don't want to hear the bullshit you feel me? Get on this Smiley…NOW rather than later." Shell said before breaking the connection.

Smiley paused for a second before he decided to let that exchange go and chalk it up to Shell being concerned for his family. He'd been friends with Tre since kindergarten and had been considered a part of the family the first time he'd met them, Tre was his A-1 since day one and so too Shell, Stance and especially Devah and that would never change so he understood that Shell wasn't necessarily lashing out at him as he was the situation. And he was right, his intuition or as his friends called it, his 'Spidey sense' never lead him astray, it was as much a part of him as his other senses and it was something that ran in his family. His grandmother and those before her were what others thought of as psychic however they termed it being in touch with their inner-most being and having a spiritual gift from God, the gift of discernment. It was a gift that was passed on to him and he didn't take it for granted, it was what made him so absolutely great at doing his job…well that and his tenacity. He'd call Shell later on when he thought he'd had a enough time to calm down and hopefully he'd have something to tell him besides the fact that he had Shay looking into it…thinking of Shay she hadn't called back yet so he decided to try her again because he need answers.

Chapter 14

Vacay Baby

Shay heard her phone ringing while she was in the kitchen trying to replenish her electrolytes before she got dehydrated messing around with her chocolate delight. Damn that man knew how to play her body like a fine tuned violin, mmph he just did something to her.

"Bae, can you see who that is for me?" she said standing with the freezer and refrigerator doors open trying to cool off.

"Smiley." He replied abruptly.

"Oh ok, I'll call him back later." She replied while pouring him a glass of Gatorade. Shay put the top back on the drink, closed the fridge and made her way back to the room wearing nothing more than her birthday suit where he was waiting wearing a similar outfit.

"Here you go," Shay said as she handed him his glass.

"Thanks, aye let me ask you something. Why is this Smiley dude all through your call log? You talk to him about as much as you do me, what's up with that? You fucking him too?" he asked before draining the cup and sitting it on the side table.

Oh boy Shay thought, here we go with this bullshit and that was exactly why she didn't do relationships, her life and the people in it were too complicated for the average man to deal with so that's why she and her playthings had an understanding, nothing personal EVER, only trivial information and conversation were to be exchanged but this one, he was different. Meaning he didn't play by the rules, for example…scrolling through her call log.

"Why, do you care? And why are you looking through my phone."

"Because I can…and yeah, I do." He responded before handing her phone over.

"Uhh, no you can't and you do what?" she responded taking her phone and sitting it on the night table, completely forgetting her rhetorical question to him.

"Care." He responded while gathering his clothes and heading to the connecting bathroom.

"What?" she asked screwing up her face like WTF are you talking about.

"You asked if I cared…the answer is yes." He responded before closing the bathroom door on the stunned look on her face and turning on the shower.

"What!?" Shay said once again utterly shocked by his response. He cared? When had that happened? She took great pains to keep her playthings at a distance, never getting involved more than sexually or occasionally for a game of pool and some drinks; all at her discretion and honestly for her pleasure and release. Yet somehow this one had slipped in and gotten comfortable without her even realizing it. Now that she thought about it he'd been around longer than any of the others, had met a few of her friends outside of her job, knew where she worked and lived and was now going through her phone and talking complete and utter nonsense…he cared, yeah right. Just 'cause he made her laugh and kept a smile on her face, could hold an intelligent conversation on a myriad of subjects, was tall and fine and could twist her insides inside out…oh shit please don't tell me I'm falling for his ass she thought as the last year filtered through her mind and she realized that one by one she'd dropped all of the rest of her companions and only HE remained on her roster.

"Oh noooo," she moaned out loud holding her head in her hands. She started running in place and shaking herself as if she could keep the feelings that had been lying dormant from reaching the surface of her brain and connecting with her heart. Finally she collapsed on the bed and closed her eyes in disbelief, how the hell did she let this shit happen? Well at least he'd saved her the trouble of asking him to leave since he'd gathered his clothes before he'd went into the shower, usually neither of them bothered with clothes unless they were going somewhere.

"You finished with your tantrum?" Jahvier asked leaning against the doorway having silently witnessed her meltdown.

Shay lay there with her arm thrown across her face, utterly embarrassed that he'd seen her display of emotion, wishing and praying that he'd take the hint and just leave before she did something stupid like ask him to stay.

"I know you heard me, but that's ok you don't need to talk, just listen a'ight. Look, I know you don't do relationships for whatever reasons and at first that was fine with me because I wasn't looking for one. I don't know what happened but around the time we went on that weekend get-away I found myself falling for you. I tried to tell myself that it was the ambiance but even when got back home you were always on my mind…your smile, the sound of your laughter, the way your face lights up when you let your guard down and actually have a good time. Hell I even love your serious face, and don't get me started on the 'I'm pissed off at you' face. But my favorite face is the one you make when I'm making love to you, my dick gets hard every time I think of it." He said as he silently undressed. "I don't know how it happened, all I know is it did and I'm tired of hiding how I feel because you're not ready to admit you feel the same." He said as he walked over to the bed and removed her arm. "Don't you?" he asked daring her to look him in the eye and lie.

Shay closed her eyes and did just that.

"I don't know what you're talking about Jah, I told you from the start that I didn't have time for a relationship, my life is way too hectic to entertain a serious commitment…"

He cut her off, causing her to open her eyes and stare at him, "And yet you've spent the last year doing just that, with no problems I might add. Look you've always been honest with me, I knew from the start that you were dating other men and like I said, in the beginning that was fine. But now," he paused shaking his head and closing his eyes, "the thought of another man touching you drives me insane with jealousy and that's an emotion I am NOT familiar with. I want us to give this a try, but if you're not willing to open up and let me be your one and only man than I'll bounce, but know this…if I walk out that door with anything less than that then I won't be coming back because I can't do this one-sided love thing anymore a'ight?" he said moving her hands above her head as he stretched out on top of her, spreading her legs with his knees as he plunged inside her all the way to the hilt, making her body jerk from the unexpected pain/pleasure it had received. His penetration made her lose her breath as she tried to run from the fullness of him sliding in and out of her but he held her in place as he ravished her, nipping on her neck and sucking on her breast all the while holding her hands, her arms stretched taut in one of his while the other roamed her body at will, covering her body with goose bumps. Shay felt her release coming as he plunged harder and faster in her wetness, her pussy making sloshing noises as she moaned his name and whimpered beneath him. Just as she was about to come, he stopped and got up.

"What are you doing?" Shay asked not believing he'd just stopped in the midst of some of the most mind blowing, raunchiest sex they'd ever shared and was standing there, sweat trickling down his mahogany skin, staring at her with his mouth moving, but she couldn't hear a damn thing he was saying she was so lost in the sexual fog he'd created.

"Shay!" he said loudly trying to get her attention.

"What! What are you doing Jah, how you gone stop just like that?"

"Because that's as far as I'm willing to go if you're not in this with me." He said softly, "Shay I want you with every fiber of my being, but if you're not feeling me the same way than I'm ghost bae." He told her before adding, "So what you gonna do?"

"Jah you can NOT be serious right now. Can't we have this conversation after we finish…"

"Naw baby girl, it's now or never."

"This is so unfair Jah, really. How can you expect me to suddenly feel something that I don't want to feel? Who does that? Just because you've suddenly had an 'aha' moment doesn't give you the right to dictate how I feel or to make unreasonable demands on my time or my life." She paused to catch her breath, her anger bubbling to the surface. "Where in the hell is all of this coming from anyway?" she asked as she climbed out of the bed to stand head to shoulder with him, head tilted back as she got in his face. "Look, you can't just change the rules and then give me an ultimatum ok? You've had months, almost six to be precise, to reconcile with what you're feeling and you've apparently come to grips with it. But you expect me to just adjust my time frame to suit you? Give me the consideration you gave yourself because at any time you could have walked yet *you* decided to stay and allow yourself to become more involved with me than either of us wanted, and certainly more than I expected. But let's get this straight…what you will not give me, now or ever, is an ultimatum. If the two of us continuing our entertainmentship or whatever this is hinges on my giving you a definitive answer or you walking out the door then so be it. I will not allow you to corner me into something I don't feel I can fully commit to or try to decipher feelings I'm not ready to explore. Do I want to be with you; for now yes, will I continue to want to do so…I don't know. I'm not good with this shit man, I don't want to fuck it or you up with my issues. Why can't we just let it be for now?" she implored, her honey brown eyes looking into his and trying to get him to see things her way. Jah thought about it and realized he was being unfair to her. She was right, he could have walked away months ago but instead he chose to stay and she deserved to be able to wade through her feelings the same way; however he was standing firm on the one man rule. He absolutely refused to share her with anyone…

Shay's ringing phone interrupted his train of thought, but only temporarily as they both looked at the phone and he saw that the object of his angst was calling yet again.

"You gonna get that?" he asked daring her not to.

"No, I'll call him back later."

"I think you should answer it, or is it you just don't want to answer because I'm here?"

"Why wouldn't I answer my phone just because you're here? If I needed to speak to whomever privately then I'd just excuse myself, I don't have anything to hide from you or anyone else."

"Why is dude being so persistent tho'? You still fucking him?" he asked heated.

"What!?" Shay asked incredulously and then she burst out laughing. The look on Jah's face sobered her up as he headed for the phone, picking it up and answering for her, however the machine had already picked up the call.

"What were you trying to prove just now? I mean really, it's none of your business who calls my phone; I do have a life you know. But just to put your mind at ease, Smiley is not nor has he ever been my lover. We're everything else to one another but that."

"What does that mean; spell it out for me clearly."

"He was my partner on the force before he left the job, he's my mentor, big brother figure, and part-time boss. He's my best friend; we've been through a lot together you know, I don't know what I'd do or where I'd be without him."

"Your boss? I thought you said he left the force."

"He did, he's a private investigator now with his own business, several of them to be truthful. I work for him on the side, in between my cases."

"Ok,' he said nodding his head thoughtfully as he realized why she wasn't always accessible to him, "so that explains why you're always busy. I used to think you were out with other men, but then I figured out that wasn't the case and shit I was so relieved I didn't really care what was keeping you so busy as long as you kept making time for me."

"How did you figure it out…that I wasn't out seeing other men?" she elaborated at his puzzled look.

"Oh that, hell I figured if you were getting it like that on the regular you wouldn't be so damn tight or so damn horny every time we got together." He said laughing as she pushed him and rolled her eyes. "But seriously though, back to the topic at hand, I see what you're saying and you're right I am being unfair so I'mma fall back and let you work it out. However I ain't trying to share you so on the off chance that you are still dating other men, I'mma need you to dead all that activity."

"You're the only person that I'm seeing." Shay responded softly. "And if I'm being honest you're the only person I want to see."

"For now." He said referring to her earlier statement.

"For as long as we both want, however long that may be." She said getting on her tip toes to wrap her arms around his neck and lift herself up on him before wrapping her legs around his hips and impaling herself on his massive dick, arching her back as she slide down his length.

"Mmhh, you sure know how to change the subject. But for real though, the next time your boss calls, I'm gonna need for you to answer so you can let him know that for the rest of the week your phone is gonna be off, hell you're on vacay baby, he's just gonna have to find someone else to call." He said as he slowly bounced her up and down his penis, spreading her open so he could go further as he lubed his fingers so he could double penetrate her…

"Anything you say bae." She moaned as she shuddered from the insertion of his finger in her ass. The sensation was so mind blowing she squirted all over him with the best orgasm she'd ever had.

Chapter 15

Star Board

Star walked on board the *CAILIN* struggling with her roll on luggage, dressed in a fire engine red two piece bathing suit with a multi colored crocheted cover-up, strappy red heels and no one to greet her. She looked around for a deck hand or anybody for that matter to help her with her luggage before her sunglass covered eyes spied a familiar face exiting the stairwell. Her hormones went into overdrive and just as she yelled his name another familiar face walked out behind him laughing at something he'd said. They both looked her way as he held the door open for Devah and she strutted through looking like a million bucks. She had on an ankle length flowing, strapless sundress in various hues of blues and teals and her feet were dazzling with rhinestones adorning her sandals and sparkling with every step that she made, her natural hair crimpy and held back with a bejeweled head band and a pair of Chloe` oversized sunglasses. Star stared at Devah with utter dislike as she watched Ra pull her to his side and wrap his muscular arm around her. As she broke the eye contact that they'd had and gazed up at him the smile they shared was enough to set Star over the edge.

"Damn Ra, it's like that? You so whipped you can't even come speak to an old friend…I thought we were better than that. I'm sure she won't mind if you help me to my room and we uh, catch up with one another." She said knowing the only way for her to get at Devah was with her words.

"Even if she doesn't, I do." He responded. "I ain't about to entertain the rest of that statement."

Devah chuckled. "I got this one bae." She said turning to address Star, "It's not that I mind, it's just that he won't be doing any of that for or with you." She stated matter of factly. "I'll order you food for you while you handle this." She said gesturing towards Star before heading off to the dining room.

"Wow, it's like that Ra? You're not happy to see me?" Star purred as she walked toward him swinging her hips from side to side, she knew her walk was mean.

"Seeing you doesn't faze me one way or the other. I see that you're still very much full of yourself." He said with a smirk.

"I'd rather be full of you." she replied as she came to a stop in front of him.

"Naw ma, that ship been sailed."

"As you can see I like to travel so I can always meet you at the port." She said tracing her finger down the front of his chest.

"Yeah, you do get around don't you?" he said grabbing her wrist and removing her finger.

"Why don't you just take a little time and think about it." She suggested while looking him up and down, eyeing the way his upper body filled out the crisp white wife beater he sported, lingering on the slight bulge outlined beneath his navy cargo shorts. "I see he's thinking about me." She said licking her lips.

"Oh, you think my dick is getting hard huh? Sorry to burst you bubble but it's actually getting soft, it only gets hard for my lady."

"Well from what I understand your uh lady can't do what I can do. I heard her skills are lacking when it comes to the bedroom." She said, embarrassment causing her to lash out without thinking.

"Oh yeah, well whoever told you that just didn't know what he was doing. You see he didn't know how to maneuver, touch, kiss, lick or dick that body like I do so if anybody's lacking it would be him." He said, knowing instinctively that Star was the one Tre had cheated on Devah with that day. "So next time you see him, tell him I said good looking out, I appreciate his lack of creativity."

"I'm just saying, word on the street is she ain't all that in the bedroom or any room for that matter. That name got her head so swollen, she believing her own hype." Star said laughing.

"Yeah well I know for a fact the streets ain't tell you no such shit. There's only one person who could've told you that, and to tell the truth…if I was a lying, cheating, grimy mutherfucker I'd've told you the same damn thing to get what I wanted 'cause that's what niggas who can't appreciate a good thing when they've got it do. Me…I'm on a whole other level, one you'll never be able to reach so how about you stay in your lane and quit trying to swerve into mine before you end up having a tragic accident." He warned her as he started to walk away.

"Like you know everyone she's been with. You niggas kill me with that shit; a bitch'll tell you what you want to hear too so go 'head with that bullshit you talking. He ain't have no reason to lie, I was going to fuck him regardless." She blurted out, again not thinking about what she was saying.

"I guess 'he' is the streets huh?" Ra laughed as he walked away holding up three fingers letting her know she'd just confirmed the truth.

Star stood their wallowing in her humiliation and anger, wondering what the hell it was about Devah that inspired such devotion from those around her and plotting on a way to dethrone the bitch just for the hell of it.

****

Quin stood listening to Star and Ra's conversation. When Ra walked away he approached her from behind startling her.

"You need any help with those bags?" he asked sensing a kindred soul in Star, someone who was just as twisted as he was and willing to go to any lengths to get what she wanted. He had plans for the Cain and Actlin families and none of them were good. He needed an ally to help him achieve his goals and with Star being family she could get access to them that he couldn't outside of job requirements. He was going to use Star to set his plans in motion and then let her take the fall when everything came to an explosive end he thought laughing to himself. Both families and everyone else on board wouldn't know what or who hit them, he'd take them all out in one big bang. After he drugged and dragged Lainy to his hide away he'd set his plans into motion. He'd already forged all of the paperwork he needed to establish new identities for both Lainy and himself he just needed someone who could tell him the ins and out of both families daily activities, under the guise of making sure everything went smoothly while they were gone and with Star he'd found the perfect patsy. He'd also use Star's jealousy of Devah to get back at her for coming back in Lainy's life and breaking them apart, because in his delusional world that's the person who was responsible for destroying all of his plans and poisoning Lainer against him and of course she had to suffer before she paid the ultimate price by losing Ra like he lost Lainy and Star would be the perfect person to use for that task as well especially since she already had a vendetta against Devah and she was clearly feeling Ra. Let the fun begin Quin thought as he followed his unknowing accomplice to her quarters.

Chapter 16

Suspicions

Devah watched as Star stared a hole in Ra's back as he walked away. Something about Star disturbed her but she just couldn't put her finger on what it was beside the obvious dislike that they had for one another.

"Here you go," Flossy said placing her orders in front of her. "That's a lot for one person in'it?" he asked.

"I ordered for Ra too." Devah replied laughing, "I know I can eat but that's a little too much for me." She said reaching for her salmon salad and ginger & orange dressing, her favorite meal as she had it almost every day, sometimes more than once in a day. "Mmhh, this is so delicious Flossy, I love you more every time I taste this for making your version of this salad for me. OMG and don't get me started on this dressing!"

"Well I appreciate the love Miss Devah, but I'm gonna have to ask you to tone it down some for that young fella of yours'n gets the wrong idea in his head and tries to take a player such as myself out of the game!"

Devah laughed so hard she almost choked. She'd known Flossy for most of her life and he was always carefree and free spirited, not to mention funny as hell. She grabbed her Angry Orchard hard apple cider and took a drink, "Man go 'head with all that Flossy, you always do this when I start eating but I am not entertaining you today, you will not have me spitting my food out or choking today. No sir, I rebuke all of that in the name of Jesus," she said putting her fingers up in the sign of a cross.

"Damn, so it's like that now? You feel the need to rebuke me for bringing some laughter into your life? Boy I tell ya…women. Y'all ain't never satisfied, even when we bring you nothing but the upmost pleasure y'all find fault."

"Awww, did I hurt your feelings? You want me to give you a kiss to make it all better?" Devah replied not buying his act one bit.

"Yeah…that'll work." He responded leaning over the bar just as Ra arrived.

"I don't even think so old man, keep them crusty soup sippers away from my lady." He said giving Flossy dap as they shared a laugh. Ra requested a Heineken to go with his meal and bit into his juicy burger, almost eating half in one bite.

"Damn, you done worked up an appetite in'it?" Devah teased Ra.

"That's what happens when you put in work. And I most definitely did that, so now I got to replenish all those calories so I can tear that…"

"Ra!" Devah said looking at him like he'd lost his mind.

"What? Flossy in the back, he can't hear me."

"Says who?" came the reply from the back.

"Oh my goodness…I can't believe you Ra. You know you can run out sometimes. Now he knows all my business and shit!"

"Hell I knew about that before he opened his mouth. I saw the two of you coming back on board last night; he damn near dragged you to the elevator. Dudn't take a genius to figure out what his intentions were especially with that dress you had on little lady."

"See, he already knew." Ra said dipping his fries in ketchup and stuffing his mouth, he took a swig from his beer before noticing the look of death that was on Devah's face.

"What?" he asked again, laughing at her.

"Oh, so it's funny right?"

"You can't blame the young buck, little lady. You knew when you put that dress on what you were doing and what was gonna happen. That's why you didn't come out of your room until it was time for you all to leave, you didn't want anyone to see you." Flossy laughed at her look of guilt. "I've known you most of your life, and I know when you're up to something. Men are visual creatures, when we see something we like, we fixate on it. You spent all night teasing this young buck with all your…visual delights and it worked like a charm. You got exactly what you were looking for. Worked out for the both of you I'd say. Hell in the end, both of you ended up coming out on top...pun intended. If you blame him you got to take some of the blame too." Flossy said clearing away the empty dishes and wiping down the counter.

"Damn, you don't miss nothing huh old timer?"

"Don't much happen around here I'm not aware of. I like to keep my eyes open to everything around me, that way when the shit hits the fan I'll already have my umbrella up cleaning up the mess."

"I feel you on that. I'on know 'bout cleaning up no shit, but yeah you gotta keep your eyes open, but yo' can you do me one favor fam and keep your eagle eyes off my lady? I'd hate for you to come up missing old timer." He joked.

"Sheeit, you'd have to be able to catch me in my sleep and since I never sleep in the same place two nights in a row, that'll be kinda hard to do." Flossy responded.

"But you have your own Quarters, why would you do that?" Devah asked forgetting her earlier ire.

"So I can keep my eyes on everything that's going on around me, and so nobody can predict my whereabouts. You can never be too careful, especially around people you don't know well like some of these new recruits. Being in the Navy Seals taught me to always trust my instincts and to never, *ever* get caught slippin'."

"Well, I'm glad we have you looking out for us but don't think I forgot all that trash you two were talking. You'n know me like that mister." She said, teasing Flossy who she knew, knew her like the back of his hand as he wasn't just an employee but also trusted friend of the family.

"Sometimes the truth hurts, but eventually it must be told. Wudn't no need for you to continue on in your delusions." He said, teasing her back with a big grin on his broad face.

"Whatever, forget the both of you. I'm going somewhere I don't have to worry about the two of you ganging up on me."

"Now that's a mighty fine visual you're givin' an old player such as myself, but as you know, you're like a daughter to me and I could never agree to such an indecent…"

"Man if you don't go 'head with that bullshit you talking." Ra responded

"That is just so disgusting Flossy on so many incestuous levels, I'm done with you for the day. I just can't." Devah said walking away. "Oh by the way, could you make me another salad please? Extra salmon." She instructed before disappearing, leaving the two men alone.

"So, why were you trying so hard to get rid of Devah? Something on your mind old timer?" Ra asked having peeped game from the beginning.

"You not as slow as you look young buck. How'd you know I wanted to speak to you privately?" he asked curiously.

"Because I'm skilled at reading in between the lines and all of that watch your back and not sleeping in the same place stuff pretty much filled in any empty spaces. What's up, what's got you so leery? Or more to the point, who?"

"I can't call it, I only know there's some foolishness going on around here behind the scenes. Sometimes I feel like we all sitting around waiting for the first shoe to drop and catch our attention while the second shoe rears back to kick us in the ass."

"Is there a particular person or persons you're concerned about?"

"Hell yeah, everybody new worries me. Some fishy shit went down a couple of month's back, a lot of good, loyal people lost their jobs behind it. As long as I've been working on the *CAILIN* ain't nothing like that ever happened, then…BOOM, overnight everything is discombobulated, folks being accused of shit they'd never do and BAM we got a whole new set of folk we got to train, live and work with. I don't know young buck but it's enough to set my antennae up so I've been watching the comings and goings of the new crew and for the most part they're alright folk, but it's one in particular…a guy goes by the name Quin. He needs to cut all that damn hair off his head and face and he keep on them damn shades, says he needs them cause his eyes sensitive to the light and shit ya know, but personally I think he's lying… something's off with that one or my name ain't Floyzelle. The reason I saw you and baby girl coming back last night is because I was keeping an eye on him. He's real shifty like, always trying to get into places he ain't supposed to be. I've seen him coming out of rooms nobody was staying in so there was no excuse for him to be there. I talked to the Jace and Sean about it and they're looking into it. Told me they would have you know who handle things on the low. I'ma keep my eye on that one regardless, and you keep your eye on my girl, 'cause I've seen him giving her looks that weren't too damn friendly if you know what I mean. And not just her either, Miss Lainy gets those same looks too, but you can't kill someone for a few ugly looks, well at least not legally so I need more than that to go on. I just wanted to make you aware of what I peeped from my observations of him. He's a cold one that Quin." He said, shaking his head and handing Ra another beer. "Shell is already suspicious of him, says Miss Lainy has been getting weird vibes from him, like he's watching her or something, which just feeds back into what I've been saying, so he's keeping an eagle eye as you said on her already… among other things." He said with a sly grin.

Ra laughed out loud, "You don't miss nothing!"

"I'm tryna tell you young buck, it's hard to catch me slippin!" he boasted sincerely. "I'ma go make your lady her salad before she gets cranky, you know how she can get."

"Shit you know her better than I do…well maybe not."

"Definitely not son."

"But you get what I'm saying," Ra said with a laugh. "I'm gonna go see if she done calmed down some. Maybe I need to make her go lay down and take a nap or something." He said with a smirk.

"Yeah right, a nap consists of closing your eyes and going to sleep not closing your eyes and going in deep playa. Now I might've been born at night but it damn sure wudn't last night young buck." He said laughing with and at Ra. "And ya better make sure Zell ain't sitting outside the door again!" he said to Ra's retreating back.

"I ain't worried about all that, I'm a grown ass man." He responded, peeping around the corner to make sure none of Devah's uncles were in sight before continuing on ignoring Flossy's raucous laughter.

Chapter 17

Flying High

"Zi, if your plan is to break each one of my fingers one by one, you're doing a great job bae."

"I'm sorry Tre, I'm just nervous. I've never been on a helicopter before." Zi responded, easing her grip on Tre's hand slightly.

"But you've been on a plane before so what's the real reason you're so nervous?" he asked.

"You think you know me so well, you make me sick..."

"Well I hope you get well soon." Tre joked, but after taking a look at her face he chilled.

"As I was saying," Zi said cutting her eyes at him as he tried to keep a straight face, "There is a big difference between a plane and a helicopter... emphasis on the word big. I feel squeezed up like we're sardines in a can or something."

"Sardines come from a can? What the hell are sardines anyway?" Tre asked jokingly.

"Tre!"

"Alright...Ok, I quit. What else Zi? 'Cause I know that's not all."

"Your parents..."

"Whom you've met before, on numerous occasions to be exact."

"How am I supposed to look them in their eyes lusting after their son? What are they going to think about us being together Tre? I really don't think I'm ready for this, we should've waited a while before springing this on them, they're gonna think I'm…"

"The love of their son's life…period."

Zi sighed and eased the pressure from his fingers some more before relaxing completely. She sat watching as her niece played co-pilot, sitting up front and following everything Curt, their pilot told her to do. She was all smiles as he let her take control of the aircraft, causing Zi to go into panic mode and grip Tre's fingers once more.

**

"Thank you so much for letting me help, I really enjoyed it."

"Anytime little lady, my daughter used to fly with me all the time. It felt good to have someone who reminds me of her flying with me. Now that she fly's her own aircrafts she don't have time to sit over there too often anymore." He said wistfully.

"Well I'm glad to know I bought you as much joy as you've bought me Mr. Curt."

"Just call me Cap, everybody else does. Mr. Curt makes me feel ancient, besides that's what they call my father." He laughed.

"Oh so you're a junior?"

"Eh, more like number five."

"Well then since everyone else calls you Cap, I'mma call you Cinco, that'll be your codename the next time we fly together." Lo said thoughtfully. "Now you have to give me a codename."

"Ok Kelona, how about Gabby?"

"Gabby? Where did that come from?"

"You, because you like to talk…a lot!" he responded laughing at her.

"Oh you got jokes right? I don't think so, try again." She said shaking her head.

"What are you two over her laughing about?" Zi asked walking up to them.

"He's trying to come up with a codename for me, I'm his new flying partner."

"Now I don't know about all of that, but yeah I've got to come up with a name that fits her. I know, how about Angel Tree?"

"What? What kind of name is that?"

"Her spirit is angelic and she likes her 'trees'…you know what I mean." They all started laughing because he was right, Lolo loved her weed, but she made sure she was never high around the kids at the center.

"I like that…Ok, Cinco and Angel Tree, team High Five!"

"Team High Five it is." Cap agreed laughing.

"Y'all two are crazy. Tre!" Zi yelled his name, heading back to him. "I am not flying back with those two nut jobs." She stated loud enough for them to hear her and double over laughing even more.

"I'm over here," he said waving her around the aircraft and right in front of his parents.

"Oh, hello Mr. and Mrs. Actlin, how are you?"

"We're good, how was your flight?" Ri asked.

"Nerve racking, between him and them," she said indicating Tre and team High Five, "I wasn't sure if I was gonna lose my mind or go crazy."

"That's like saying 'Is you done or is you finished?'…it's the same thing."

"Not for me. FYI, you would rather me lose my mind than to see me go crazy." Zi stated seriously. "You've been duly warned."

"Apparently so." He said leaning down to give her a kiss.

"Tre…" she said, slightly nodding her head towards his parents.

"So let me get this straight, you just threatened me in front of them but you're worried about kissing in front of them?"

"I didn't threaten you, I just gave you a heads up and yes dammit, they're your parents!" she whispered.

"You do know that they're standing right there and can still hear you right?"

"Yes, we can and since you're being so shy all of a sudden, as if we haven't known you've had a crush on Tre since you were in the 6th grade if not before or that he's been pining for you since you first moved away and he had to find out through Devah. He was so crushed…"

"Ma, chill. Dad can you please do something with your wife?"

"She's your mother, you do something…I'm good over here." His father responded, putting his arm around his wife's shoulders.

"What? I'm just pointing out the obvious, you two were meant to be. Welcome to the family for the second time." Ri said giving Zi a hug.

"Thank you Mrs.…."

"Ma, just like the rest of my girls call me. And who's this beautiful young lady with my favorite pilot?"

"That's my niece Kelona, we call her Lolo or Lo for short. Kelona, this is Tre's parents Mr. and Mrs. Actlin."

"Hello dear, it's nice to finally meet you, you are simply gorgeous. I'm Ri but you can just call me Auntie Ri. Since Zi is your auntie, I'll be one too and later on you'll meet my best friend and your other pseudo auntie Londa, call her Lonnie." Ri said, knowing she was wrong for setting Lo up like that. Jace was the only person who could call her Lonnie, anybody else and Londa would firmly and effectively put you in your place. She'd be there to make sure Londa knew she was the one who put her up to it, so she would know not to go in on her for the faux pas.

"Do not follow that woman up young lady, you may call me Auntie but if you call me Lonnie we gon' fight, I ain't scared of either one of you beautiful creatures." Londa said coming from the front of the helipad. "This auntie," she said pointing at her bestie, "is being a mean girl and trying very hard to make me lose my cool but it ain't gonna work chica. I'm too blessed to be less than my best." She said giving Zi a hug. "Hey sweetie, I see you decided to join us. Wonder what…or better yet who changed your mind." She joked. "And hello, I know I just got finished talking trash to you but I do that to everybody so don't take it personal. Just know and please believe I meant what I said tho. What's your name?"

"Kelona, but everyone calls me Lolo or Lo. And trust me, I believe you." She said reaching out to shake Londa's hand.

Londa knocked her arm away, "So this is the young lady you're always talking about Zi. Girl you better give me a hug and act like you know. I don't play that Sugar Honey Iced Tea, give me some love honey bun."

"Zi, I really like them. You might have some competition for my niece-ly affections." Lo said giving Londa and then Ri a hug.

"Hey don't forget about me, the ladies can duke it out all they want to but I'm your new favorite Uncle. Uncle Sean is my name, welcome to the family Lolo. Zi has mentioned you a lot over the years. So much so I feel like I know you and you better be ready to drop some fire come Talent Tuesday, Spoken Word Thursday and/or Soulfessions Sunday."

"Ok, the first two I'm familiar with but that third one…is that a fusion of Soul and Confessions?" Lo asked.

"Exactly, see she got it." He said looking at his wife who shook her head at him.

"I got it too…it still sounds corny to me so what's your point?" she said causing the rest of them to laugh.

"It is kinda corny dad."

"You could've left kinda out of it." Londa told Tre drily.

"Boss, I see where you going with that but…nah bruh." Cap said running his hand over the top of his bald head while shaking it.

"I like it Mr. Actlin."

"Me too." Zi co-signed.

"Thank you ladies, and it's Uncle Sean to you and you already know Zi."

"Yes sir."

"Ole' brown nosing heifers." Ri said eyeing the two young ladies.

"Fo' sho." Londa concurred. "Come on so you can meet the rest of the family Lo. Tre, why don't you show Zi to your room and we'll get Lo settled in hers."

"Oh no, I'm not sleeping in the same room with Tre, I'll share the room with Lolo." Zi said nervously. There was no way on God's green earth that she would allow anyone to even think that Tre was dicking her down like he did in her dreams…no-WAY!

"Well no one said you had to sleep dear." Londa said walking away with Lo in tow and Ri laughing beside her.

"OMG, your aunt is too much for me Tre."

"You know how she is, stop fronting. Besides she's right, you don't have to sleep. We could stay up all night just…"

"Tre I…you…don't you dare."

"What? I was going to say talking, but I like what you were thinking about much better." he said with a smirk.

Zi turned around and walked away.

"Where are you going?"

"Away from you and yes I'm dead dog serious right now." She said causing the men to all start laughing.

"I'd better go find her before she gets lost."

"You do that son."

"Thanks for coming to get me and dropping us back off Cap. See ya next time old man."

"No problem son."

"Old man…Son? Something you two wanna tell me?" Sean asked looking at them.

"Yeah, I think you and mom got a few things to work out pops."

"Sheit, no offense Curt, but ain't a nigga alive can step in my shoes when it comes to that woman there. Take your jokey behind on after that young lady before she finds someone who can do more than make her laugh or make her mad, 'cause it looks like that's all you got going for you right now."

"Like you just said but in my own words…I ain't worried about nothing you saying pops. I got that." He said walking away to go find his lady.

"Now that he's gone, what's going on Cap? You're usually right back off once you've finished so you can pamper that beast over there, unless of course you're still needed."

"When we were flying in, I noticed a black box under the waterline on the rear starboard side of the boat, there's also a rope ladder hanging from the side. Now I might not be the brightest candle in the set, but I ain't the dimmest either. You need to have somebody check into that immediately and make sure you do it on the low. Somebody aboard this yacht is up to no good and until this is figured out and my mind is at ease, I'm staying put in case you guys need me and my services. I also have Dee Dee on standby with some of her friends. That's what took me so long to join you guys. I didn't want to alarm the women and I also wanted to inform you solo."

"I need you to check that out for me." Sean said out of nowhere.

"I fly, I don't dive." Cap replied.

"I wasn't talking to you Cap. Let me know the minute you know something." Sean said before giving Cap his full attention again. "My apologies, I was talking to Smiley, Tre's friend."

"Yeah, I remember him."

"Right, he's doing some undercover work for us so the minute you started talking about seeing something attached to the boat, I turned my communicator on so he & Jace could hear what you were saying and get right on it. He'll discreetly inform those who need to know and do what needs to be done. Thanks man, most people would have missed that, but not you Captain Eagle Eye Hawkins."

"Luckily the water was clear, 'cause these eyes aren't as sharp as they use to be but I can still hang in there with the best of them."

"Curt, good to see you my man." Jace said walking up to the pair.

"Good to see you as well." Cap replied clasping hands and giving Jace a one armed hug.

"I heard the message. What in the hell is going on around here? I'm at a complete loss, not to mention all the shit that happened before we even set sail."

"I know, nothings adding up but I get the distinct feeling that the shit is about to hit the fan, so we need to be on the look out and make sure we keep our women out of this shit storm that's brewing."

"I agree."

"I'm with you guys, just let me know what you need me to do."

Sean and Jace took Curt to their briefing room and filled him in adding yet another strong ally to the family's side.

Chapter 18

Getting Down Low and Dirty

Smiley immediately contacted Flossy and the two of them came up with a game plan. Their main suspect was Quin and since it was two of them against what they hoped was just one they deduced that it would be easier for Smiley to keep an eye on Quin while Flossy, who knew how to handle such covert missions would go see what kind of foolishness they were facing…in his words. While Smiley went about his way, tracking Quin he noticed that he was either always around talking to Star or watching Lainy from a distance. Smiley thought about what he was seeing and allowed his inner being to sort through the smoke and mirrors to reveal the truth to him but it was all still too fuzzy around the edges and soft in the center. Until he could form a whole picture, he'd keep his thoughts to himself and his partners. Just because he was in tuned to his third eye didn't mean he couldn't use several other pairs when his was occupied, such as now. Smiley saw Ra come around the corner with Devah behind him. He noticed how Star's face lit up when she saw him and then went sour once she noticed Devah. Not good, not good at all. Now he had another thing to add to his plate. Devah kept going to the bar no doubt to pick up her usual Salmon salad, but Ra stopped to use the restroom. When he looked to where Quin had been just a few moments before, he was nowhere in sight and Star was creeping towards the men's restroom.

"Fuck my life." Smiley said with a frown before calling reinforcements and heading towards the bar. "You should head to the men's restroom before someone gets hurt." He warned Devah on his way Starboard to make sure Quin didn't head that way and telling Shell and Tre to see if they could locate him.

"Nothing over this way." Shell said in his ear.

"I got him." Tre responded letting the other two know where he was and what Quin was up to.

"Is he injured?" Shell asked.

"All I know is he's in the infirmary and doc is on her break so there's no one in there with him."

"Look, I'll be there shortly, do not go in there behind him Tre. Wait for us," Smiley warned.

"Now where's the fun in that? You know I'm your huckleberry Smiley." He said quoting the line Val Kilmer made famous as Doc Holiday in the movie Tombstone and also meaning that he was just the right person for the job.

"Tre, just wait for us, I'm almost to you now." Shell said in his ear.

"Good, I'll see you when you get here." He said ending the conversation and turning his earpiece off.

Tre walked toward the infirmary, when he reached the door it was slightly cracked so he took a peek inside before pushing the door all the way open, startling Quin in the process.

"Hey, what's going on? You working for Doc now?"

**

"Hello…Tre? What the fuck? Did he hang up Shell?"

"I believe so." Shell responded.

"We need to get to him quick and in a hurry. You never know what a motherfucker will do when his back is against the wall." Smiley advised.

"I'm walking down the hall now." Shell said, making his way to the infirmary.

"Wait for me." Smiley said exiting the elevator and walking toward Shell. "Why your brother so fucking hard headed?"

"You tell me, he's your best friend." Shell responded.

"Bruh, that's *your* fucking brother." Smiley pointed out.

"Well we can't help who we're related to." Shell said as they reached their destination. "And even if we could I would never trade any of my siblings in for all the money in the world…no matter how much they get on my nerves."

**

"Nah bruh, I was just looking for something I left earlier…" Quin tried to explain before Tre cut him off.

"You're looking for this something in the medicine cabinet? I guess it's a good thing that doc keeps it everything locked up tight, 'cause the way

149

you were trying to get in there tells me you looking for more than what you're saying." Tre said pulling his card.

"Man look, my bad. I got a little confused bruh, won't happen again." Quin said looking for a way to get out of his predicament. He'd been looking for drugs he could use to knock both Lainy and Shell out to make it easier to carry out his plans, but now Tre was in his face minding his business and there was no way in hell he could let him know what he was really after. "I'll just come back when doc is in." he said trying to ease past Tre.

"Yo, where're you rushing off to so quick?" Tre said blocking his exit. "Doc'll be here in a minute and you can ask her where your…my bad what did you say you left again?" he asked knowing full well that Quin had never mentioned the mythical object.

"Damn man, I said its all good so why you sweatin' me?" Quin barked not knowing Tre well enough to know that he was feeding right into his brand of fuckery. He lived for that shit, pissing people off to get them off centered while he pushed their buttons. It was the quickest way to get someone to inadvertently show their hand.

"Bruh what's with all the loud clapping you over there doing?" Shell directed at Quin as he and Smiley entered the room having heard the loud voices from down the hall. He looked dead at Quin as he spoke, if it ain't directed it's not respected so he wanted him to know who he was talking to.

"Aye, yo listen…I'm just trying to leave so I can get back to work. Your brother won't let me through; I'm trying to find out why so fall back my nig." Quin said trying to bluff his way out of the situation he was in. "It don't even matter what his problem is, I'm out." He said attempting to get past Tre and not realizing that even if he stood a chance of doing so, he'd never make it past the other two.

"Well check this my man, you ain't going nowhere unless this situation right here is resolved to my satisfaction. I'm your boss, you work for me nigga not the other way around so don't get shit twisted. Now when I came in here, you were trying to get into a locked medicine cabinet but yet you're gonna lie to my face and tell me you left something earlier like I'm trippin' and shit…I'm not. But since you left something, we gonna make sure you get it, doc should be on her way back from her break so we gon' just chill until she gets here. Fuck what you talking about." Tre informed Quin in warning. Quin didn't heed the warning.

"You didn't hire me so unless Mr. Actlin or Mr. Cain tells me differently, I'm out."

"Nigga is you stupid or is you dumb?" Tre asked laughing. "You got two Mr. Actlin's in here so like I said…you ain't going nowhere." He antagonized Quin and he reacted just as expected, he threw a punch at Tre but before his fist could connect Tre had already jabbed him right between his eyes, giving him an instant headache and causing him to see so many stars he never saw the two hits that followed. One busting his nose and the other landing him on his ass.

"What in the world is going on here?" Dr. Ellen Morre asked walking in on the beat down. "Tre, what has gotten into you, and why are you two standing around watching instead of stopping him?" she wondered aloud looking at Shell and then Smiley as she stood between Tre and Quin. "Ok, start talking…somebody better tell me something real quick before I start digging up in all y'all asses. And y'all know y'all don't want that so let's hear it." She finished, arms crossed over her breasts, leaning back on her left leg with neck tilted to the side and her right eyebrow raised.

Chapter 19

A Devah in Control

Devah turned around and looked toward the restrooms where she knew Ra had gone and then glanced at where Star once stood and put two and two together

"That little grimy bitch gonna make me hurt her." Devah said on her way to the restroom.

"Who are you talking to sis." Shane asked walking up to her with Lainy, Zi and Lo in tow.

"Your attention seeking cousin that's who."

"What in the world has she done now, knowing you don't fuck with her like that and you ain't wrapped too tight?" Zi asked laughing.

"I'll find out in a minute." Devah responded continuing on towards the men's room. "She better pray she ain't where I think she's at."

"Ok, you've officially gone off the deep end of a short pier. You mean to tell me you're ready to hurt her for using the restroom?" Lainy asked puzzled.

Devah reached her destination and pulled open the door.

"Uhm, sis…that's the wrong bathroom." she said walking behind Devah only to see something she wished she could un-see.

"Ohh Tres…" Star moaned, on her knees in front of Ra who had his hands in her hair pulling tight. His back was to the door but he knew the moment Devah walked in and he knew what it looked like. There was no way Devah was going to believe anything he had to say after what she'd been through already. The rage that filled Ra was so great he didn't realize that he had thrown Star back into the trash bin until she yelled out in pain, landing sprawled open with all eyes except the ones she wanted focused on her.

"Devah, I promise you on my life, this is not what it looks like."

"Oh but it is though. It's exactly what it looks like." Devah replied.

"It most certainly is, Ra you don't have to lie like that. I told you her record speaks for itself, she can't satisfy you like I can, that's why you pulled me in here in the first place. So I can do what she can't, her reputation for being stuck up and bougie both in bed and out precedes her. I tried to warn you last time we were together but you didn't want to listen."

"Yo, if y'all don't get this nasty ass tramp up out of my face I'ma do something to her I ain't never done to a woman." Ra said focusing on Devah who was focused on Star. "Man bae, she lying, on everything I love that ho wasn't sucking my dick. When I walked out the stall she was standing here naked. I tried walking past her but she grabbed my basketball shorts and pulled them down before I could stop her. When she grabbed my dick I pulled her head away from me before she could do anything and that's when you guys walked in. Look at me Devah…I told you before, if you want to know something just ask me, I'ma always keep it real with you. Fuck keeping it 100 there is no limit when it comes to me and you."

"So if I wasn't sucking your dick then how did you get that lipstick on it?" Star smirked, looking at Ra's meat still hanging from his pants, he'd forgotten to tuck it in and since Devah was standing in front of him he didn't think the other ladies had seen him as he tucked himself back in his pants.

"The fact that you got lipstick smeared between your thumb and forefinger might explain that. Either way you ain't 'bout shit Star, how could you do that? Why would you play yourself over another woman's man? What's wrong with you that you always want what belongs to someone else? I know auntie taught you better than that, ain't you 'shamed? I know I am, your momma would be too disappointed if she could see you now. That man don't want you, get over it and while I'm thinking about it…was I the only one who heard her call out another nigga name when we first walked in?" she asked curiously.

"Naw, I heard that shit loud and clear." Lainy replied.

"Me too. So it was you all this time?" Devah said, looking at Star.

"You knew Ra was interested in me before he met you so yes it was me all this time." Star shot back venomously.

"Look you delusional bitch, for the last fucking time I AIN'T NEVER NOR WILL I EVER FUCK WITH YOUR THOT ASS." Ra said very distinctly making sure she understood every word that left his mouth…loud and clearly. "I warned you before to stay in your lane and stop trying to swerve into mine. That's how shit get fucked up and people get hurt. Get your fucking life and stay the fuck outta mine."

"I wasn't talking about Ra…that's not whose name you called when you were down there trying to suck on what belongs to me."

"So you believe me bae? Thank you, I wasn't trying to lose you behind no bullshit like this, I ain't trying to lose you period."

"I know. Can you please excuse us for a minute? There are a few things I need to holla at Star about right quick." Devah said finally looking at Ra and giving him a smile.

"Wait, whose name did she call? Once I realized what she was trying to do I kind of lost it so I didn't hear anything."

"She called the nigga who was cheating on me with her…Tres. Damn, you had all that in front of you and you still couldn't get your mind off Tres? That nigga must've held it on you boo. I'ma give him his props, he was good, real good but he could never top the immense joy and extreme pleasure I receive from this man right here. That's something you'll never get the satisfaction of experiencing with another woman's or more specifically…my man. All you'll ever be to another woman's man is his side piece, his jump off, his dick warmer. You'll never reach wife status playing Merry Go Round with every nigga you set your sights on. That's some free advice from me to you. Now if everyone will excuse us, we can have that conversation I was talking about earlier."

"Devah…"

"Ra, go…please. This has been a long time coming and since she keeps sending for me I'm here, now let me see what she wants a'ight?"

"Shane, so you just gonna let her fight me? You know she'll listen to you, why you always putting her before me? I'm your real family, I'm your fucking cousin…you mean to tell me you ain't gonna help *me*? Who the fuck does that…where they do that at?"

"Yes. I know. Because she's loyal and she loves me and she would never put me in this type of situation and then beg me to get her out of it. Family is what you make it and she's been more family to me then you ever have. And what? That is correct. Me and right here…right now." Shane ticked off each answer on her fingers. "Ladies, sir let's let them chat; I'm sure they both have a lot to get off their chests." Shane said holding the door open for everybody to exit. She looked at her best friend and sister and she didn't have to say a word.

"Don't worry Shane, I won't." she said knowing that although Shane would always be in her corner, Star was still family so she wouldn't hurt her too bad, but she was gonna hurt her, you could bet that.

Chapter 20

Secrets Revealed

Lainy sat at the table waiting for Shell to join her. On their way to the dining room, he'd gotten an emergency call from Smiley and he told her he'd join her as soon as he could. She'd been waiting about 20 minutes so far trying to figure out how she was gonna tell Shell about Lain & Lona. She didn't know what the outcome was gonna be but she knew she had to do it, she just didn't know when. She was so deep in thought that she didn't notice Ri standing in front of her calling her name until she tapped on the table just as Lainy had decided to wait 'til they got back to SC to tell Shell. Lainy jumped, startled.

"Oh, I'm sorry! I didn't see you, uhm Shell had something to do if you're looking for him. He said he'd join me when he was through."

"And I'm sure he will, but that's not why I'm here. Do you mind if I join you? Shell is gonna be a little longer than he thought according to his father so he sent me to keep you company. Have you ordered yet?"

"No ma'am, I was waiting on him to join me first. But you can go ahead and order and you don't have to worry about keeping me company, I think I'll just go lay down for a while." Lainy said sliding to the edge of the booth, preparing to leave.

"My son wearing you out huh?" Ri said laughing at the look of shock on Lainy's face. "Oh chile please, you're the mother of his children…why wouldn't you be tired, twins are a handful are they not?" she asked quietly.

"I…Wha…Uhm…"

"You're trying to figure out how I know; I have my resources. Smiley is like a dog with a bone when he sinks his teeth into something. We're alike in that way, he and I. I couldn't figure out what you were so afraid of, or what you were hiding but I knew it was something and so I put him on it and imagine our surprise when he turned up not only birth certificates but adoption papers as well. Were you ever gonna tell my son about his children or were you gonna let us going on walking in the dark, oblivious to your lies and deception?"

"Mrs. Actlin…"

"So formal…Ma, remember?"

"It feels a little awkward calling you that right about now to tell you the truth."

"Which you seem to be having a hard time with right now. Talk to me Lainy, why would you do that to us? Have we ever given you a reason to believe that we wouldn't accept you or your children? Have we ever not treated you as family? Help me to understand why you would hurt my son like you're gonna end up hurting him when he finds out, and make no mistake he is going to find out. I had to pull all kinds of rabbits out of my hat to keep Smiley from telling Shell. It finally boiled down to the fact that since I hired him to find the information he couldn't reveal what he'd learned without breaking my confidentiality. But with that being said, if you don't tell him I will."

"You don't have to threaten me Mrs....Ma, I was planning to tell him once we got back. That's what I was sitting here thinking about when you walked up. And for the record I never lied to Shell about the twins, I just never told him."

"A lie of omission is a lie none the less Lainy."

"You're right, and I am sorry. I just didn't know how to come out and tell him. I never thought I'd have to. The night I got pregnant with the twins was the best night of my life. I was so in love with Shell, but somehow our signals got crossed and I didn't want him to think I was trying to trap him by getting pregnant. Once I found out it was two instead of one, I just packed up and left. My aunt and uncle were going to raise them as their own because they can't have kids and I didn't know what to do with one much less two babies but I couldn't give them to complete strangers either. I was in a real messed up place back then. I was trying to finish school, keep up my grades and I didn't know…I just made some fucked up decisions and I really hope they don't bite me in the ass once I tell Shell."

"Shell loves you, he might be upset at first but I have faith you guys will work it out. Here's a little bit of advice, if you want to be with my son you're gonna have to learn to not only love him but trust him too. Trust him to be the man his father and I raised him to be and stop fighting him, let that man love on you like a real man is supposed to." Ri advised her. "And another thing, I apologize for poking around in your business but know this, I'm a wife first and a mother second but nine times outta ten the lines become real blurred, and when it comes to my children I don't do blurred lines a'ight?"

"Yes ma'am, I hear you and thank you for coming to me first and letting me do this my way. As a mother I know your first instinct was to tell him what you learned, I'm glad you didn't because if it comes from anyone other than me I might just lose him forever."

"Actually my first instinct was to kick your ass for keeping my grandchildren away from me and having the nerve to be around my family and I constantly without ever having said a word. Hell I just might still do that, but for now I'ma chill. Just know that that option has only been moved to the back burner and reduced to a simmer. Now show me some recent pictures of my grandbabies before I change my mind."

Lainy laughed as she pulled out her phone, put her password in, and pulled her pictures up, handing Ri the phone. As Ri was perusing the photos they heard a loud scream come from the direction of the restrooms. Star emerged screaming and threatening to have both Ra and Devah arrested and looking every bit of the clown Devah made her up to be when she smeared Star's infamous lipstick all over her face and hair. Even with the fucked up makeover her closed, swollen eye that was slowly darkening and her busted lip shined through.

"What in the world...who did that to Star? Let's go see if she's alright!" Ri urged as she slid to the edge of the booth she was sitting in, intent on finding out what had happened and making sure the person responsible paid for it. She didn't really care for Star, but she didn't want anyone being attacked while they were under her family's care...especially not a woman.

"Uhm, you might want to sit this one out."

"Now why the hell would I do that Lainy, that's just cold hearted."

"No, that bitch right there is cold hearted. She waited in the bathroom while Ra was in there, stripped down, grabbed him and tried to…give him head." She said, her face on fire. "Devah walked in and trust me whatever Star planned backfired on her. Devah asked us to excuse them so they could have a long overdue conversation. I'm guessing we're witnessing the end of that conversation now. In case you didn't get all of that, your daughter did that." Lainy said laughing at the look of shock on Ri's face.

"You have got to be fucking kidding me. My baby did that?"

"No your grown ass daughter did that." Lainy corrected before getting up and walking over to Star, snatching the phone out of her hand and then hanging it back up.

"What do you think you're doing? Move out of my way before I add you to my list!"

"Bitch please, I ain't near worried about you. What *you* need to be worried about is what the fuck *I'ma* do to you if you don't make yourself disappear from this yacht by tonight and leave my girl and HER man alone. Now you can either catch my drift or you can be set adrift…which one works for you because I'm good with both of them, either or?"

"This is my family's boat, if anybody is gonna put me off it won't be your irrelevant ass. You think just because you fucking Shell you run something?

Trick please, sucking dick don't get you no brownie points around here."

"If anybody should know it would be you now wouldn't it cousin? What's going on here?" Shane asked joining the group.

"This chick talking about calling the police on Devah and Ra like she don't know we in international waters. These people don't play out here!"

"Like I give two fucks, I am going to have them arrested before the night is over."

"If you decide to do that then you're gonna force my hand and I'm going to have to send auntie the pictures and videos we took of you on your knees in front of Ra and sprawled out on the floor when Ra tossed your ass to the trash where you seem to like it since you like acting like a gutter bitch. And you and I both know what happens then; all these trips, all the shopping, all the cash is gonna dry up quicker than that weave dripping toilet water all over you."

"But I didn't even do anything…"

"It don't even matter whether you did it or not, that's not what the pictures are gonna say." Shane said with a smirk.

"Little girl, if you think for one minute I'm gonna let you bring unnecessary drama into my child's life you are sadly mistaken. I will annihilate every single thing about you before I'd allow that to happen. So if I were you, and thank God I'm not, I'd listen to Lainy and promptly make myself disappear. And that's from someone who gets plenty of brownie points for sucking dick but since I run shit around here, I don't need to use them on you." Ri said quietly but firmly.

"Oh shit, what the hell have you done now?" Londa asked walking up and stopping beside Ri to put her hand on her shoulder and calm her down.

"You'n even wanna know." Her daughter answered.

"It don't matter what she did, she got to go…end of story." Ri answered.

"'Nuff said." Londa responded before motioning one of the crewmen forward. "Make sure she gets all of her belongings and escort her from our presence pronto and the boat as soon as we get to port."

"Auntie…"

"Who?" Londa swung her head back in Star's direction with her eyebrow raised quizzically. "I've been knowing you over 2o years and not one time have I ever heard you call me auntie. Chile boo, don't even try it, carry on."

"I wish I had never set foot aboard this ship."

"No what you wish is that you had never fucked with me." Said Devah, "I've given your ass pass after pass because I never wanted to cause conflict between my family and yours. But what I've realized over the years is that my family and your family are one and the same. And instead of you recognizing that and embracing it you chose to bring drama and conflict. And then you wonder why nobody wanna fuck with you. I would advise you to get your fuckin' life before you ever try to step to me because believe me if you send for me again, I'm coming and you ain't gonna like it when I do. Trick you better act like you know."

"Bitch you think you all that…"

"And she is, now be gone before I hurt you little girl. My daughter played with you…I'm not about to." Ri warned.

"Oh shit, auntie gangsta!" Lo whispered to Zi.

"See this is why I don't let you out the house…you don't know how to act." Zi whispered back.

All of a sudden there was a loud commotion heard in the distance.

"What the world is going on?" Londa asked headed toward the source of the sounds.

"No Londa, we don't know what's going on. Let me call Sean."

"You call Sean, I'm going to find Jace…" Londa replied.

**

"Doc, did he leave something in here earlier?" Smiley asked, cutting straight to the chase. His spidey senses were going off and he knew things were about to finally come to a head.

"No, I haven't seen him all day. Why would that cause you to beat on him like that TreSean?" she asked curiously.

"That's not why I spanked him Doc, he swung at me first so I had to learn him." He said with a smirk at Quin.

"He swung at you first...soooo now what, we back in third grade now?" she asked eyeing her childhood classmate.

"Nigga you ain't did shit, fight me one on one and see what happens." Quin unwisely and ignorantly taunted.

"One on one? Who you think beat your ass the first time?" Shell asked. "Damn bruh you must've been moving hella fast, this nigga think you ganged him all by yourself!" Shell cracked causing everyone to laugh and giving Quin the in he needed to finally get a hit off on Tre...too bad he didn't count on Ellen being quicker and popping him from the side with a jab to his jaw.

"Damn El Boogie, you still got it." Tre said referring to the healing hands that back in the day used to lay the boys out for pulling her hair and later on the hormone induced teenagers who learned real fast they could get a fatty for touching on her fatty. When you're the baby girl in a male dominated family of boxers, it came naturally.

"It is what it is, now get this asshole outta my clinic and lock him up until we get back home. I don't trust him; anybody who has to sneak someone to gain an advantage gets no love from me." She said frowning up her face at Quin for that bitch move.

"Let's go." Smiley said moving forward to apprehend Quin.

"Nigga...you'se a fucking cook, get the fuck outta here!" Quin laughed, still out of it from the blows he'd taken and pissed because he hadn't landed one yet. Third times the charm...or not. He swung on Smiley who grabbed his hand in midair, twisted under it and bent it behind him before 'accidently' shoving him into the wall and cracking his front tooth causing even more blood to spew from his face.

"FUCKKKK!" Quin yelled from frustration and pain. "Y'all niggas some straight pussies! Y'all can't do this shit to me! I ain't did nothing, he can't prove I did shit so y'all better let me go if y'all know what's good for ya. And you," he said referring to Doc. "you shouldn't've ever put your fucking hands on me. I'ma make it my business to see that you lose your license, believe that bitch!

"Show of hands...did anyone see me stick this bitch ass nigga?" El asked while checking the medicine cabinet. Not one hand went up, she didn't even bother to check and see if any did, she just knew. "That's what I thought. On the other hand, I see damage to my cabinet. It looks like someone was trying to break in it. Anybody saw who did that?" she asked, this time looking at Quin as each one of them raised their hand although only one of them actually saw him. Knowing he didn't have a leg to stand on he tried to run out the room and got football tackled by Shell who bashed his head into the floor before allowing Smiley to take over and cuff him. Unfortunately he chose the wrong kind of cuffs, he should've had the plastic ties because Quin had a set of handcuff keys in his pocket for the set he planned to hog tie Lainy with when he kidnapped her.

"FYI...I'm a detective, I own my own PI business and I take bitch ass niggas like you off the streets for fun." Smiley responded to Quin's earlier statement as to who he was. He snatched Quin up off the deck expertly and pushed him towards the elevator. Quin laughed as Smiley lifted him up off the floor.

"Y'all niggas ain't fuckin' with me! Y'all can't see me, this shit right here is a minor setback, y'all niggas ain't ready for this major comeback tho!" he yelled as they walked down the breezeway, headed for the elevators laughing and screaming like a madman…well actually like the madman that he truly was.

Before Londa could get to Jace, the elevator opened up and a bloodied and bruised Quin staggered out with Smiley, Tre and Shell behind him. Smiley held a gun pointed toward him as he gave orders to his men to lock Quin below in one of the rooms and stand guard until they arrived back in the US and he could be apprehended at the first port they arrived at. While everyone was wondering what was going on, Quin was busy loosening his restraints. Smiley's spidey senses started going off but it was already too late, Quin snatched Smiley's gun and rushed over to the women. Grabbing Lainy and putting the gun to her head, he dragged her backwards isolating them from the others and unknowingly making himself a bigger target.

"If you want to see her brains sprawled all over this deck then by all means, go for it." He threatened Shell who had started running toward them.

"Qua?" Lainy questioned, easily recognizing his voice now that he made no attempt to disguise it.

"The one and only babe. Did you really think you were going to get rid of me like that? Come on, I invested way too much time and effort in you to let you get away from me like that Lay." Qua said quietly in her ear while keeping his eye on the men in front of them. Seeing Shell standing there ready to take his head off prompted him to antagonize him by licking Lainy's neck and biting on her ear. When she head butted him with the back of her head he slammed the gun across the side of her face...Shell instantly saw red.

"Don't do it bruh, he wants you to lose it. Don't let him get to you, you know where her heart is." Smiley tried to soothe the beast lurking beneath the surface of Shell's skin.

"I'ma kill that sick son of a bitch when I get my hands on him."

"Not if I kill him first." A voice said from portside as a red beam landed between Qua's eyes. "Any last words?" Stanley Morrison asked. Lainy's eyes widened when she saw her father step into view.

"Dad? How'd you know where I was? What are you doing here?" she asked temporarily forgetting about Qua as she tried to head for her father, that's when he knocked her memory back in focus while also guaranteeing himself a nice eternal sleep with the fishes.

"You know you're gonna pay for that right?" Stanley asked taking a quick glance at the blood dripping down his daughter's face. "Lainer, do you remember the game we used to play with your mother...she's in my ear telling me to tell you hi by the way, anyway do you?"

"Hi Ma," Lainy replied before answering her father's question. "The weight game?" she guessed correctly instantly knowing what he wanted her to do.

"Yeah sweetie, that's the one. You think you can..."

"So you two think this is a waiting game? Well guess what, time is up! We all fixin' to lose! I'ma blow this bitch to smithereens!"

"I hope you're not talking about with this." Flossy said walking up to the gathering, soaking wet, dripping water all over the deck and holding up the casing to the now deactivated and destroyed bomb. Knowing he wasn't going to make it out of this alive he played his last hand.

"Yeah a'ight," Qua replied, knowing without a doubt that his time had just expired as he'd planned to use the threat of the bomb to get away with Lainy. "Y'all got that, I know I ain't long for the living but before I go I just wanna say…I'll see you in hell." He said pointing his gun and shooting Shell just as Lainy let her weight go, dropping down and getting out of the way as the bullet from Stanley's gun put a hole in his head.

"Nooooo!" Lainy screamed, first crawling and then running toward Shell's body lying on the bloodied deck.

THE END

For now anyway! Stay tuned for Part 3 of Homies, Lovers & Friends coming in 2017!! It was a joy writing this book and if you haven't already purchase part 1 of this series Homies, Lovers & Friends: The Beginning, where it all began. Until next time...peace, love and happiness.

Dawn Diva

Made in the USA
Columbia, SC
22 April 2025